D0829024

"I haven't felt this good

That voice. Those hot, needy words.

Patrick's kiss grew deeper, hungrier. It invited reckless decisions and wild sex, sweet soreness come morning and—

His phone jingled and buzzed, and Steph shot up as if she'd been zapped by a Taser. She stared around the dim room. How long had they been kissing? Ten minutes? An hour?

Patrick looked equally surprised. He cleared his throat and dug his cell from his hip pocket.

"Hello?...Hey, John....Excellent, hang on. Head to the end of the hall—the door to the gym's at the bottom of the stairs....Yup, I'll stay on."

The strain of arousal lingered in his voice, but he covered the more incriminating evidence handily, strapping on his tool belt around his hips as he left the room.

Steph blew out a long breath. What had she done?

Nothing. *You kissed an electrician. At work, granted, and on the night you were supposed to be kissing a doctor.*

Bad, bad, bad, she thought, and licked her tender lips, still flushed from Patrick's demands.

Bad, bad, bad, and way too good....

Blaze®

Dear Reader,

Here we are again, back in the heady basement confines of Wilinski's Fight Academy! If you joined me for rounds one and two, then you've met some of the men of the gym already. But are you ready for Wilinski's first resident female fighter?

Steph's stepped into the ring with some tough opponents in her day, but nothing's prepared her for the threats that Patrick poses—a thump in the nose, a hammer to the hand and, before long, a carpenter's big, rough fingerprints all over her carefully guarded heart.

I hope you'll enjoy watching this lovable working-class charmer dismantle Steph's best-laid plans for a whirlwind romance with one of Boston's urbane elite. I certainly enjoyed writing their romance. Most anyone will tell you, I just can't resist a man with capable hands and steel-toed boots.

Happy reading!

Meg Maguire

Driving Her Wild

—

Meg Maguire

PROPERTY OF
J. CAMPBELL LIBRARY

(H) HARLEQUIN® BLAZE™

If you purchased this book without a cover you should be aware
that this book is stolen property. It was reported as "unsold and
destroyed" to the publisher, and neither the author nor the
publisher has received any payment for this "stripped book."

Recycling programs
for this product may
not exist in your area.

ISBN-13: 978-0-373-79777-6

DRIVING HER WILD

Copyright © 2013 by Meg Maguire

All rights reserved. Except for use in any review, the reproduction or
utilization of this work in whole or in part in any form by any electronic,
mechanical or other means, now known or hereafter invented, including
xerography, photocopying and recording, or in any information storage
or retrieval system, is forbidden without the written permission of the
publisher, Harlequin Enterprises Limited, 225 Duncan Mill Road,
Don Mills, Ontario, Canada M3B 3K9.

This is a work of fiction. Names, characters, places and incidents are
either the product of the author's imagination or are used fictitiously,
and any resemblance to actual persons, living or dead, business
establishments, events or locales is entirely coincidental.

This edition published by arrangement with Harlequin Books S.A.

For questions and comments about the quality of this book,
please contact us at CustomerService@Harlequin.com.

® and TM are trademarks of Harlequin Enterprises Limited or its
corporate affiliates. Trademarks indicated with ® are registered in the
United States Patent and Trademark Office, the Canadian Trade Marks
Office and in other countries.

Printed in U.S.A.

ABOUT THE AUTHOR

Before becoming a writer, Meg Maguire worked as a record-store snob, a lousy barista, a decent designer and an overenthusiastic penguin handler. Now she loves writing sexy, character-driven stories about strong-willed men and women who keep each other on their toes...and bring one another to their knees. Meg lives north of Boston with her husband. When she's not working on her next book, she can be found in the kitchen, the coffee shop or jogging around the nearest duck-filled pond. Visit her at www.megmaguire.com.

Books by Meg Maguire

HARLEQUIN BLAZE
608—CAUGHT ON CAMERA
734—THE WEDDING FLING
740—MAKING HIM SWEAT
762—TAKING HIM DOWN

To get the inside scoop on Harlequin Blaze and its talented writers, be sure to check out blazeauthors.com.

Other titles by this author available in ebook format.
Don't miss any of our special offers. Write to us at the following address for information on our newest releases.

Harlequin Reader Service
U.S.: 3010 Walden Ave., P.O. Box 1325, Buffalo, NY 14269
Canadian: P.O. Box 609, Fort Erie, Ont. L2A 5X3

My inevitable thanks to Ruthie—
as essential to my writing as a keyboard and coffee.
Which I suspect was her evil plan, all along.

For Charlotte—I lay this BDToF at the feet of the
master, eager to incite your womanly stirrings.

And my thanks as always to my editor, Brenda,
whose headshot hangs dead-center behind the
Lucite on the Wilinski's wall of fame.

_1_

STEPH PAUSED AT THE BOTTOM of the steps, gym bag in hand, and gave the space a long study. Wilinski's Fight Academy.

It wasn't how she remembered it from her last visit, in November.

It looked like a bomb had exploded.

The cardio equipment and mats and the boxing and octagonal rings were crowded to one side, the other half overtaken by milling contractors and stacks of cinder block.

In the fighters' corner—the sounds of gloves whacking and men grunting, the bass din of the hip-hop that fueled their drills.

In the workers' corner—shouted questions and directions, the squeal of a band saw or sander from inside the space that would become a second locker room in a couple weeks' time. A thick sheet of rubber flaps hung over the would-be door, but dust still escaped.

Sweat and concrete—the scents of laboring men.

Steph had sampled enough of each to last a lifetime. The next time she got close to a guy, she hoped to heck he smelled like a gentleman. Whatever gentlemen smelled like. Cedar, maybe, or citrus or leather, or that stuff from Hermès that she'd bought for her older brother one Christmas. Robbie had taken one sniff and made a face, so she'd snatched it back, promising to get him Bruins tickets instead. Now the bottle lived in her bedside drawer, and occasionally she spritzed it on her pillow and pretended it was evidence of her incredibly urbane boyfriend, out of town in Brussels, attending a convention for surgeons or dignitaries or CIA operatives—any job that came with really sophisticated Christmas parties, so she'd have an excuse to wear heels and curl her hair.

Someday. Somehow.

For now, here she was in a gym, construction dudes on one side, fighters on the other, a big old buffet of the kinds of guys she used to date. Perfectly nice ones, likely. Good, hardworking men like her dad and brothers and her friends and exes from Worcester. But she was in Boston to start a new chapter, one that might feature a boyfriend with soft, strong hands and a college degree and a knowledge of Scotch.

And one who wouldn't be embarrassed to introduce her, saying, "And this is my girlfriend, Steph, the retired cage fighter."

Yeah, good luck with that.

She toed off her sneakers and tucked them in one of the cubbies by the door. Giving the construction chaos a wide berth, she headed for the workout area, scanning for a familiar face. She found one, its owner busy leading a group in kickboxing drills.

Rich Estrada. She'd met him at a big event in Vancouver the previous spring, and she ought to sue him for emotional distress, for hoisting her hopes up to such dangerous heights.

The first time she'd laid eyes on him, he'd been dressed for a press thing, sauntering around in a suit. He didn't have a fighter's face—not yet—and she'd been intrigued. The kind of sophisticated guy she *never* crossed paths with. The event had been held at a huge casino, and she'd assumed he was some jet-set high roller visiting from the Riviera or someplace. She'd been in for a shock the next day when she glanced to her side and found him whacking a heavy bag in the gym. And when they'd spoken—that accent. He sounded like every guy she'd known growing up, dropping all his R's and sticking extra ones where they didn't belong. The most elegant man she'd ever seen, and he winds up being Boston disguised as Barcelona.

He called a water break now and she caught his eye, waving.

"Penny! Hey."

She winced. She'd been fighting as Penny for ages, a nickname from when her baby brother hadn't been able to pronounce "Stephanie." It had stuck because her hair was red as copper, and she'd competed as Penny beginning with her preteen karate days. Since then it had followed her through her first true love, judo, then jujitsu, then on to mixed martial arts. It was time she put her foot down. Here and now she'd quit being the person everyone imagined she was, and start being who *she* wanted to be.

"I prefer Steph," she reminded Rich.

"Sorry, I knew that. Steph. Welcome home."

She looked around, nodding. "This'll do."

"Don't say that. You're here to help us haul this dungeon out of the dark ages. Make Wilinski's into Bahstan's premieh gym for mixed mahtial ahts," he said, making fun of his own accent.

"I'd have thought that was your job, Mr. Celebrity." She sighed, frowning her commiseration. "Sorry about Rio." He'd lost his title to Vicente Farreira a couple months earlier in Brazil, under suspect circumstances. "If the organization doesn't run a doping investigation on Farreira, they're in for a shit-storm. Nobody's build changes that much—not dropping *down* a weight class."

Rich shrugged. "The controversy's been good for me. Got a match in August with a payday that'll keep me from bitching about pretty much anything. And months to prepare."

"Nice." Steph could appreciate how luxurious that must feel. The female side of MMA wasn't nearly as popular, and with fewer major events, she'd often taken offers with less prep time than was ideal, not wanting to miss an opportunity. But now she was retired—from the stress of the road, if not the sport. At the moment she felt relieved, though she knew in time she'd probably miss the focus that came with a match on the horizon. Though not as much as she'd come to miss feeling grounded the past couple years.

She'd be thirty in less than three weeks, and was ready to start working toward goals that hadn't mattered until recently—a place of her own, a taste of real dating, a relationship, a family down the road. Her aggressively autonomous twenty-three-year-old self would've laughed, but Steph apparently had a biological clock. And it had begun to tick, if softly. A rough loss and a stress fracture had officially cooled her commitment to the pro life. She'd managed to never break anything worse than her nose and a few toes all these years, and for the first time ever, she realized she might like to keep it that way.

Rich whistled to call the members back from their break. "Get in on this, if you want," he told her.

"Just let me change. Am I still in the lounge?"

He nodded.

"'Fraid so. But until our female membership takes off, you'll practically have that new locker room all to yourself once it's finished. Though I'll warn you, it's tiny. You wouldn't believe the loopholes we had to squeeze through to even get planning permission to retrofit it."

"I'm sure it'll do."

She crossed to the room beside the gym's office and

closed the door. There was no lock, so she pushed her bag against it, rooting through her workout clothes, swapping her winter coat and jeans for warm-ups and a jog bra. She tugged on the latter, untwisting the straps as she dug for a top. Then—*bonk*.

The door was shoved in, whacking her in the nose.

"Ow, Jesus!"

No matter how many times she took a punch there, the startling, white pain of it never got easier. She cupped her hands to the spot as she straightened, suddenly face-to-face with one of the construction guys. His recognition dawned slowly.

"Oh, sorry. Did I just thump you in the head?"

"Yes." She drew her fingers away. When his blue eyes widened, she glanced at her palm, covered in blood.

"Holy shit. I'm sorry. Uh, here…" He muscled his way through the half-open door, toppling the contents of her gym bag, tools from his canvas belt clattering and clanging against the metal frame He unbuttoned his flannel work shirt, offering it to Steph.

Not wanting to drip blood on her own clothes, she wadded it against her nose.

"Sorry," he said again. "I didn't know anybody'd be in here. I'm supposed to wire your new TV." He nodded to a big box leaning against the wall, splashed with a picture of a flat-screen. "I'm the electrician."

Preoccupied with pressing her bridge, scouting for a break, Steph didn't reply.

"Should I get on with it, or…?"

She abandoned her nose, spreading her arms to showcase the rather obvious fact that she was dressed in her bra. "I'm kind of changing, here."

"Oh jeez. Sorry."

"Never mind." Steph wasn't modest. She'd changed in far less private venues than this, and once a warm-up banished the January chill from her muscles, she'd be back down to her bra for training. "Just shut the door and get on with it."

He did, sidestepping the mess he'd made of her clothes. "I won't look," he assured her, busying himself with the box. "Just pretend I'm not here."

She checked to make sure the bleeding had stopped, then tugged on a long-sleeved compression top. She cast her hapless assailant a glare as he crouched to organize TV components on the carpet.

He looked like every guy she'd taken shop class with in high school, the very epitome of Massachusetts working-class guyhood. Sandy brown hair that managed to look messy despite its short cut, caramel-colored Carhartt pants, work boots, a forest-green tee whose front Steph was positive would bear the logo of a contracting company. The cotton was pulled taut between his broad shoulders, but she was through being seduced by such sights.

She knew this guy too well already. He'd have a truck parked along the curb outside with a Sox decal on one side of the rear window, Pats on the other. He grilled a perfect burger and owned a large, happy dog, and played touch football with his buddies on the weekends, come rain or snow. His name was Ryan or Mike or Pat or Brendan. Brendan Connolly, Doyle, McCarthy, McAnything. Sully, Smitty, Murph. His hands felt like sandpaper and his skin smelled of Lever or Zest.

She knew these things, because she'd already dated this guy ten times over. Guys as comfortable as a broken-in pair of sneakers, but Steph wanted something more. She wanted to be swept off her feet, not pulled onto the couch for an afternoon of *SportsCenter,* with Coors-flavored makeout sessions during the ads.

"My name's Steph, by the way," she said, angling to learn his.

He kept his eyes on his task. "Sorry again, about your nose, Steph."

"I've got a shirt on now."

He turned and got to his feet, the promised logo from J.T.'s Contracting greeting Steph. He was tall, six feet or so, and had a handsome, honest face, the kind that advertised a man's every emotion. Strong jaw behind a couple days' stubble. And those blue eyes were so…*blue*. Steph wanted to slap herself for even noticing.

The guy frowned, squinting at her nose. "It's not broken, is it?"

She shook her head and tossed him his button-up. "Just a nosebleed. I've had worse." Though usually she at least got paid for it.

His eyes rolled back with relief. "Oh good. I mean, not good. But you know."

"I know." She cocked her head at him. "What's your name?"

"Patrick."

Of course it is. "I'll see you around, Patrick. Maybe next time you'll knock."

"I will, don't worry. Again—sorry. Seriously."

He wore the guileless look of a scolded puppy, and Steph felt some annoyance lift. She offered a half-assed smile and turned away, tucking her gym bag in the corner.

Rich spotted her as she approached the mats, dark eyes widening. "Jesus, what happened to your nose?"

"Your electrician punched me in the face with a door."

"You punch him back?"

She smirked. "Thought I'd save that for the ring."

"Is it broken?"

"No. Just tell me if it starts bleeding again." Steph could sense the well-groomed professionals forming an orderly queue outside the gym, just dying for a chance to woo such a glamorous woman as she.

Rich asked her to take the lead on grappling drills and she was relieved to find Patrick gone from the lounge when she went to pull on her *gi*. Wilinski's didn't have a proper jujitsu program yet—her arena, now—but she did her best with the ragtag group of uniformless members.

If the guys were feeling weird about having a woman in their ranks, they didn't show it—no leering, no skepticism. Some men could be royally macho pricks, but on the whole, fighters were a sensitive group. Theirs was a humbling, emotional sport, most of the bravado reserved for the cameras.

She'd had better offers than Wilinski's, money- and profile-wise, but there was something appealing about the challenge. She could step in as it went co-ed and feel like a part of the evolution, feel invested and valued. Feel *rooted* to something after way too many years of going wherever the fights were. Stability, after all that transience.

Once the lunchtime sessions wrapped, Rich showed her around the office and the computer system.

"Mercer's better with this crap," he said, frowning as he clicked through folders on the laptop. Mercer was the gym's general manager.

"His wife owns the dating service upstairs, right?" Spark—a slick-looking operation whose glass-fronted office shared the foyer with the gym. The most mismatched neighbors in small-business history.

"His fiancée," Rich corrected, managing to find and print the form he'd been looking for. "Jenna Wilinski."

"Wilinski?"

"Her dad opened this place in '82. She inherited both floors."

Her brows rose. "The plot thickens."

"She nearly gave the gym the chop, but luckily Mercer managed to seduce her away from reason."

"I'd have thought that was your job."

He grinned. "I know, right?"

"Doesn't your girlfriend work up there, too?" If memory served, the woman was refreshingly down-to-earth, compared with all the glammed-out girlfriends-of-fighters Steph had met over the years.

Rich nodded, fetching the papers the printer had spat out. "It's all very incestuous around here. Must be in the water."

She held in the questions she was longing to ask, knowing Rich was the kind of guy who'd tease her mercilessly if she gave him the ammunition. *So is she good, this matchmaker? What sort of guys might she find for a chick who's spent the past decade scrapping in chain-link octagons? Would I look dumb for even asking if she'd want me as a client?*

Steph had grown up an hour's drive from here. She didn't know anyone in Boston, not outside this gym, and didn't have the first clue how to go about meeting the kind of men she'd like to date. She was useless at the bar scene, given what a teetotaler training turned one into, and didn't relish taking up tango or speed-dating or going it alone on some freebie personals site. If she was going to find a boyfriend, she'd do it the right way. Do it through a service that attracted sophisticated, grown-up men who were looking for something serious. Spark might be the perfect solution and a worthy expense, provided she could muster the balls to ask.

"Autograph this," Rich said, handing her a safety waiver. "And Mercer's got tax and payroll forms for you, too, someplace." He rummaged through a filing cabinet and Steph read and signed all the papers.

"So, how you settling in?" he asked, relaxing back in the chair. "You find a place you like?"

She shook her head. "Only a sublet. A nice one, but I have to find an apartment of my own by March first."

"Bummer."

"No, it's fine. I couldn't afford this place on my own for more than a couple months."

Rich knocked her papers into a tidy stack and slipped them in a folder. "My girlfriend's looking for a roommate."

"Oh yeah?"

He cocked an eyebrow at her. "Bear in mind, I'd be your neighbor, one floor down."

Incestuous, indeed. Rich as her coworker, roommate's boyfriend, neighbor? That was a *lot* of Rich Estrada. But it was a better lead than she'd found elsewhere.

"On the plus side," he went on, scribbling *Need copies* on a Post-it and sticking it to the folder, "you'd pretty much have the place to yourself." No doubt. Rich didn't seem the type to suffer an empty bed. "Though there may be a surly teenage girl crashing on Lindsey's couch all summer," he added. "I'm paying her little sister's way to come train. If and when she graduates high school."

She smiled at that. "I'd never have pegged you for the mentoring type."

"Me neither. Anyhow, we'll have you over some weekend, and you girls can see if you mesh. It's in Lynn. Do you drive?"

"No. I sold my car when I knew I'd be moving to Boston."

"You could catch a lift with me, when we're on the same shifts. Plus there's the bus and the train."

"Sounds doable." Steph wasn't opposed to a roommate—she'd shared a million tiny motel rooms with perfect strangers. And she wasn't really opposed to living in the same building as Rich. Brash or not, he made her laugh, and most of the conversations they'd had on the road over low-sodium, fat-free training meals had been dominated by his laments about missing his Colombian mother's cooking. She wouldn't pass up an invite to an Estrada family dinner.

"I'll fix something up," he said. "Maybe next weekend."

When he stood, Steph took his lead and they headed back into the gym.

There was a mid-afternoon lull—no structured sessions, everyone doing their own thing. Steph wandered around, introducing herself, stepping in to hold targets or spot the guys working out with weights. Mercer arrived at four, freeing Rich to head home.

Steph smiled and shook Mercer's hand. "Hey, boss."

"Hey yourself, new girl." He gave her nose only the briefest double-take. "I guess you didn't find your right mind and back out, after all." Mercer was a good guy. A few years older than her and Rich, with a stern, no-nonsense face, scarred up from his years as a boxer.

"I like a challenge," she said.

"Clearly. The next class starts up at five. You need a break? Grab a snack or a drink or anything?"

"Wouldn't hurt." Also wouldn't hurt to go ahead and ask what she hadn't been able to, with Rich. "Your fiancée owns the matchmaking business upstairs, right?"

"Yeah. Why?"

She felt herself blushing, which given her complexion meant she was already red as a brick. "Is it only for business-type people, or...?"

Mercer's less-scarred eyebrow rose. "You want to join Spark?"

She bit her lip. "Maybe."

"Good for you. I'm not sure what the exact criteria are, but you can go up and ask Jenna yourself. I know her last appointment's already done for the day."

"What? Right now?"

"We're going out of town for a few days on Friday, so no time like the present."

"But looking like this?" She waved to indicate her bra and shorts, the hair at her temples and nape curled with sweat. Lord knew what her tender nose might be looking like by now.

"Ah. Maybe throw on some warm-ups. But she knows what a mess we are, on the clock. Don't worry about that."

Maybe not, but after Steph changed into yoga pants and a zip-up, she splashed her face with water and wrapped her hair in a bandanna. On the way out she made eye contact with the electrician, who was installing some device by the exit.

"Looks better," Patrick offered brightly, gesturing at his own nose.

Damn it, he was good-looking. Had this been five years ago, Steph would've already succumbed to a terminal crush on him, dolt or not.

He's been sent to test you, with his big arms and blue eyes and stubble, and his tool belt all slung around his hips. Ooh, his hips. But she'd dated this man before—over and over and over—and it never worked out. It'd be the dating definition of insanity to fall again, expecting different results. The time had come to start picking with her brain, instead of…other parts.

She glanced at his project.

"New security system," he explained proudly. "State-of-the-art. No more keys, same as in the foyer."

"Great."

"It's so fancy I'm not entirely sure what I'm doing."

"That's very reassuring."

"Not really my specialty, but hey—any work's good work in this economy, right?"

"Right." She made for the doors, sidestepping the tools and plaster chunks cluttering the floor.

"Hang on, let me—"

He tugged at a tangle of thick orange extension cord, just in time to catch Steph's ankle and send her stumbling to her knees and elbows, the meat of her hand slamming into the claw-end of a hammer.

She swore as the pain bolted through her wrist and arm, jerking away as Patrick tried to help her up. "Don't."

He hovered awkwardly as she made it to her feet. "I'm so sorry."

"I'm getting really tired of hearing you say that."

"Sorry," he repeated, oblivious as ever.

Steph studied the damage, blood beading along a nasty scrape on her palm.

"Oh shit," Patrick said. "Lemme find you something to—"

"I'm fine."

But Patrick fished in his pockets and found a crumpled, if clean, Dunkin' Donuts napkin, offering it to her.

You are… You are just so exactly who you are, aren't you?

Good ol' Pat from Boston or Brockton or Woburn, with his electrician's license and steel toes and his daily stop at the Dunkin' drive-through. She took the napkin, wrapping it around her cut and skirting the mess. She didn't dare stay in this man's orbit another second. He'd probably manage to set her hair on fire.

He called, "Sorry, Stacy."

"It's *Steph*," she shot back.

"Sorry."

She jogged up the steps, imagining running into her dream man as he left Spark. Tall, with dark hair, crisply pressed shirt, warm smile, smelling of oak.

And her with a swollen nose, bleeding hand, dressed for a jog and stinking of the effort. *Please let there be no men around.*

She was in luck. Through the tall windows that faced the stylish foyer, she spied only a woman at a desk, typing on a laptop. She'd caught sight of Rich's girlfriend on a previous visit to Boston—she had dark blond hair, so this brunette must be Jenna.

Steph approached the open door, more anxious than she'd ever felt stepping into the ring. She knocked timidly on the frame.

Jenna glanced up. "Hello!" She stood and rounded her desk, dressed in a smart skirt and tall boots, all shiny bangs and pink cheeks and white teeth. "Welcome to Spark. How can I help you?" If she was weirded out by a sweaty woman showing up in her threshold with no appointment and a bloody napkin in her fist, she hid it shockingly well.

"Hi, I'm Steph Healy. I just started working downstairs."

"I figured that had to be you. I'm Jenna. I own Spark, and I'm engaged to Mercer."

"So I hear."

Jenna went in for a shake but Steph kept her hands clasped, letting Jenna see the napkin. "Little mishap."

"Oh goodness." Jenna frowned and grabbed a water bottle off her desk, wetting a tissue. "Give it here."

After a moment's hesitation, Steph crumpled the napkin and offered her palm.

"Ouch," Jenna said, dabbing at the scrape. "If this is Mercer's fault I'll be chewing him out. Your first day and already you're all banged up."

"I had a run-in with one of the contractors."

Jenna fished in her purse and tore open a Band-Aid. It wouldn't last long once Steph was gloved and working out, but she politely let Jenna fuss.

"He's the reason I got this, too," Steph said, pointing at her nose.

"That was quite a run-in."

"They were separate incidents."

Jenna's eyes widened.

"He's not a very good contractor," Steph offered.

"Apparently not." Jenna tossed the bandage wrapper

and leaned on the edge of her desk, waving at a nearby chair. Steph sat.

"It's so good to meet you," Jenna said. "Mercer's been wringing his hands for months, convinced you were going to change your mind."

Steph smiled. "He told me. But I like it down there." Dangerous electricians aside.

Another woman appeared then—Rich's girlfriend, Steph was nearly positive.

"This is Steph, from downstairs," Jenna said.

"Oh right! Welcome to the building." She came forward for a shake. "I'm Lindsey. Is your nose okay?"

"Yes, it's fine. Nice to meet you."

Lindsey wore slacks and a deep purple sweater over a dress shirt. This seemed to bode well. Both Mercer and Rich had managed to land themselves polished, professional partners, despite their vocations. She stole a quick glance at the engagement ring twinkling on Jenna's finger, and some hybrid of jealousy and hope sparked in her belly.

"Just here to say hello?" Jenna asked. "We must look really dull compared to the action downstairs."

Steph shrugged. "Feels like I've been living in gyms the past ten years." She gave the office and its modern furnishings an appreciative scan. "This is exotic, trust me."

"Rich said you're from Mass," Lindsey said, sitting on her desk.

"Worcester."

"Nice. I'm from Springfield. Jenna's a California transplant, but even she was technically born here."

"It's hard to stay away." Steph had traveled all over—South America and Europe, Asia and Australia, and until a couple years ago, she'd thought she'd never settle in New England. Then some instinct had kicked in, like a salmon getting called back up the river. "I just moved to Fort Point." She liked her temporary neighborhood, a collection of old factories and brick office buildings straddling the border of Boston and South Boston, only ten minutes' walk. Twelve if the icy headwind off the harbor was really blowing.

"You just retired from fighting, right?" Lindsey asked.

"Yup, all done." Steph seized the segue. "I got sick of all the traveling. I'm ready to get rooted somewhere. Settle down."

"Nice."

"Rich said you're looking for a roommate."

Lindsey nodded. "I am. I feel stupid paying rent for a two-bedroom when I'm hardly ever there. You in the market?"

"Yeah. Rich said I should come over some weekend, see if it's a good fit…?"

"Great! Beats wading through the weirdos I might find online."

Excellent. One bit of matchmaking accomplished. Now, how to broach the second? Thankfully, Jenna wasted no time in steering them there.

"Do you have a boyfriend here?" she asked, eyes wide and eager.

"No. But I'd like to find one. Or at least get back into dating, now that I'll finally be in the same city for more than a couple weeks at a time."

"Well," said Lindsey. "*We* can help with that."

But Jenna's smile had faltered. She didn't seem to agree.

"I wanted to ask how Spark works. And how much it costs, all that sort of stuff?" Steph held her breath.

Jenna nibbled her lip.

"It's okay," Steph said, wanting to offer her a polite out. "If you're not taking new clients, or…"

"It's not that. I just honestly don't know if I'm allowed to let you join."

Steph's heart sank. She knew she should have changed.

She was probably wrecking Jenna's swanky cachet by even sitting here.

"Technically you're my employee, since I own the gym," Jenna explained.

"Oh." That was a small relief. Though still a let-down.

"Would you let *me* join the gym?" Lindsey asked Jenna.

"I hadn't thought about it like that." She frowned. "I'll have to call the head office. But if it's kosher, of course I'd be happy to have you."

Steph's mood brightened. "I wasn't sure if… I know Spark is for professional types."

"You're a professional ass-kicker," Lindsey said. "Plus Mercer's your employee," she added to Jenna. "If we're talking about inappropriate workplace poaching, here."

Jenna rolled her eyes and spoke to Steph. "I'll be frank—I don't know how our male clients would react to the prospect of a date with a woman who fights. But I think you'd make a very interesting addition, and I'm sure I could find you *some* matches…if not as many as I might for a woman with a more, um…traditional job."

"I figured." Her profession tended to divide guys into a few distinct camps. The insecure jerks liked to call her femininity into doubt. The perverts suggested she might want to wrestle with *them,* preferably naked and covered in oil. And the polite but not-into-it guys smiled stonily and immediately ceased viewing her as girlfriend material. But one thing had long ago become clear—the majority of men didn't relish dating a woman who could best them at chin-ups.

"I've found it challenging myself," she admitted. "I'd be fine if you marketed me as a martial arts instructor. That's technically what I am now, and I think it intimidates guys less."

"Do you know what you're looking for?"

Did she ever. "A nice, grown-up, professional guy.

With a half-decent car and some kind of dress sense." She pictured that hopeless Patrick guy, and all the other incarnations of him she'd dated. "Somebody moderately sophisticated." Who'd take her to a nice restaurant instead of the corner bar, so she could dress up and feel girly after all these years of training and touring. A man who'd make her feel like a lady, not a *chick*.

"I'll call the powers that be first thing tomorrow morning," Jenna promised. "Give me your number and I'll let you know the verdict."

She scribbled it on a Post-it, feeling hopeful. As she handed it to Jenna she said, "I promise if I get a date with one of your clients, I won't go dressed like this, or all banged up. I'm just on a coffee break, and I knew you were closing at five, so…"

Jenna waved the excuses aside. "If any two matchmakers are sympathetic to the hazards of your job, you're looking at them."

"Okay, great. Fingers crossed. I better get back downstairs."

They said goodbye and Steph jogged down the steps, mindful to approach the double doors with caution. In her absence, Patrick had moved his debris and tools to the side, and she hurried through the threshold, half expecting to trigger an explosion.

The dangerous man in question was at the other end of the gym, standing beside another worker at the emergency exit, scratching his head as they stared at a mess of wires spilling from an electrical panel.

God help him, Steph thought.

He was one of those men who just floated cloddishly through his life, helped along by those endeared by his good looks and hapless charm. Probably had sympathetic teachers who'd passed him so he could stay on the hockey team. Likely was coddled by girlfriends even after he'd forgotten their birthdays three years running. She knew his type well enough to make these wild assumptions—her younger brother was exactly the same. The lovable, harmless oaf.

She touched her nose. Well, perhaps *harmless* wasn't quite the word for Patrick.

Steph loved her brother too much to feel bitter toward this kind of man, but a part of her did find it unfair. She'd had to work three times harder than any man in her field to be taken seriously, had to push herself to succeed, since so few people at the top of the MMA food chain cared to invest their energy or resources on a female fighter. Women didn't get juicy coaching deals or promotional opportunities, not the way the guys did, and Steph's biggest payday for a professional fight had probably been as much as what a guy like Rich earned before he'd even signed with an organization.

She was a hard worker and she loved her job, but she was tired of struggling financially. She hoped she'd find an equally driven man, someone in a competitive—if civilized—field, who could offer the financial security she'd been missing her entire life.

Her family had been pretty poor, her father losing a good job as a machine mechanic when his factory was bought out in the nineties. After the layoff, Steph's mom had started working behind the deli counter at their local supermarket to supplement their income "until things picked up." Two decades later, she was still there.

Once upon a time, they'd been able to pay for Steph's first karate classes without a care, but those days were short-lived. If she'd pushed herself to excel—at karate, judo, jujitsu, MMA—it was because being an overachiever had garnered her favoritism. The kind that had allowed her to keep coming to classes at a discount or in exchange for doing odd jobs around the dojo. Martial arts had never been a simple extracurricular to Steph. She'd loved it the way other girls loved horses or ballet or boys. And she'd fought to keep it in her life.

Still, she'd been doing this for over twenty years. She was *tired*. She'd never grow weary of the physicality of the sport, but the financial struggle… She was ready to leave that behind her. Wanting a man who could offer that wasn't shallow—it was practical.

She eyed Patrick as she stripped out of her warm-ups.

Handsome, to be sure. Sexy even, and probably perfectly sweet despite the alarming frequency with which he caused her bodily harm. But even if her blood quickened at the sight of him, her rational brain knew what a guy like Patrick would bring—more struggling, little stability. Maybe a great sex life, but that wasn't a fair trade-off, not if it came at the price of all that uncertainty.

She wound medical tape around her injured hand and pulled on her gloves, ready for the evening's first workout. Down here it was business as usual—physical strain, sweat, satisfaction. Beyond these walls, though, things could be different. *Would* be different. A sophisticated man waiting for her at a restaurant, maybe kissing her cheeks, if that happened outside the movies. She'd let him teach her which wine went with which dish. Show her how it tingled to kiss a man who tasted of burgundy or merlot.

"Son of a—"

Steph whipped her head around at the sound. It was Patrick, of course. His averted cuss had accompanied an unmistakable *zap!* and a flickering of the lights. He shook out the hand he'd shocked. "Sorry!" he told everyone who'd turned, flexing his fingers. "My bad."

At least it wasn't me that time.

He was over it in a moment, back to joking with his colleague.

God help you, she thought again, watching him.

And God help the poor woman who falls for you.

2

STEPH WAS WORKING early the next day, and during lunch she checked her voicemail, finding a message Jenna had left at nine-thirty. The woman was as good as her word. She sounded chipper, asking Steph to swing by Spark when she had five minutes. Heart thumping with cautious hope, Steph jogged up the steps, smoothing her hair.

Both matchmakers were in the office, eating sandwiches off brown deli paper.

"Oh," Jenna mumbled through a bite, chewing impatiently. She swallowed and blurted, "It's you! Yay!"

"Hey, it's me."

Lindsey waved, also preoccupied with her lunch.

"Good news," Jenna said, beaming as she dabbed her mouth with a napkin. "Turns out you are allowed to join Spark, if you so wish."

"Yeah?" Steph couldn't hide her smile. Even if the service cost an arm and a leg, it wouldn't burst her bubble. "That's great."

Jenna nodded. "I just can't give you preferential treatment and I have to disclose to any potential dates that you and I are affiliated."

"That doesn't sound too bad."

"It's not. And actually, if I can speed you through the application process, I have a man who'd love to meet you for a drink tomorrow night."

She blinked. "Tomorrow? Wow, you're good."

Jenna laughed. "It was a little flukey. He's a brand-new client, and I wound up emailing him last night with some follow-up info, and we had a little back-and-forth. Anyway. He's a doctor."

Steph nearly gasped. *Play it cool, Healy.*

"Sports medicine," Jenna continued. "He works with a lot of the hockey players over by the Garden. He likes active women and I happened to mention I may have a client coming on board who's a fighter, and he was very intrigued, to say the least. Plus he says he likes redheads."

"Hey, two for two."

"Is thirty-six okay?"

"Yeah, fine by me." An older man. Sounded heavenly after all these years surrounded by twenty-something dudes. "Is he cute?"

"No," Lindsey interjected. "But he is *ha-a-nd-some.*" Her eyes rolled back in dramatic rapture. The girl ought to know handsome—she was dating Rich Estrada. "I saw his photo. He's hot."

"I haven't even signed up and you found me a hot doctor who's okay with my gig?" Steph asked Jenna. "Are you a sorceress?"

"I can't legally let you see his picture until you're a client. And technically I don't think I'm allowed to bait you with as many details as I have. But would you like to sign up? He has to work late tomorrow, on site for a game, but he'd love to meet you before he goes out of town for the weekend. The game's over around ten. Would drinks after that be too late?"

She considered it. "I could probably swap for the closing shift and meet him someplace in between." She wasn't an early bird, anyhow. And for a chance with a hot, sporty doctor? "Does my nose look presentable?" It was still tender, but she'd lain with an ice pack on it for an hour before bed and the swelling was way down.

"Much better," Lindsey said, nodding.

"Okay then. Sign me up."

Jenna assembled a stack of forms and Steph scanned them. The membership was pricey, but the decision felt right as she handed over her credit card.

"And, submit," Jenna said, clicking something on her computer. "Welcome to Spark!"

With that scary first splash into the deep end accomplished, it was time to start paddling. "What should I wear on this date?"

"Depends on the bar, I suppose." Jenna's eyes narrowed. "But it's supposed to snow tomorrow, so I don't think anyone can fault you for dressing sensibly. Maybe some fancy jeans and a nice sweater?"

Damn, Steph had some shopping to do. Her closet was seriously bipolar—sweats and sneakers on one side, a couple of short, glitzy cocktail dresses on the other, procured for the wild after-fight parties that had become her only excuse to wear heels these past few years. She owned exactly one pair of jeans, and they weren't fancy by any stretch of the imagination—not unless a hole at the corner of the butt pocket was this season's hottest trend.

Downstairs, she fairly floated through the afternoon sessions. Her final match had been three weeks ago, and she could feel the effects of her lighter workouts. She'd put on a couple pounds and lost some definition, but she didn't mind. She liked having a strong, trim figure, but it was nice to feel a little softness coming back, the perennial aches and pains fading. She was a fighter, but she was a woman, too, and could handle forfeiting her jiggle-free backside if the pay-off was an extra cup size.

"So," she said to Mercer, as they wiped down the heavy bags after a cardio session. "Guess who's got a date tomorrow night."

"That was fast."

"I know. But it's not until late. I'm happy to take the closing shift, if that's helpful to anybody."

"I'll be on a plane to California tomorrow night," Mercer said.

"Oh right, you mentioned that."

"My former protégé's got a match in L.A., then we're visiting Jenna's folks. So I guess it's up to Rich. When are you on 'til?"

"Seven."

"Friday's sparring—Rich won't volunteer to miss that… Just come in at two and I'll give you both the closing shift. I can cover the morning by myself."

"If you're sure."

He grinned. "Heaven forbid I get in the way of anybody's romantic plans. Especially if they've got Jenna's fingerprints all over them."

Excellent. Now all she needed was a decent outfit.

Mercer eyed her. "I bet some guys can be real dicks about the fact that you can beat them up."

She smiled grimly. "Some are. But they're not always nasty to my face. The worst date I ever had was with this guy I was practically half in love with, after knowing him only a few hours. He seemed *perfect.* But then…" She had to laugh, looking back on it. "This man tried to mug us, and I wound up choke-holding him."

Mercer laughed. "Nice."

"Like, in a dress and heels. I had him on the ground for twenty minutes, and my date had to call the cops."

"And did he ever ask you out again, after that?"

She shook her head. "He said he would, but nope. Not a peep."

"Do you wish you'd just let the guy mug you?"

"Nah. I'm proud I'm not defenseless."

"You ever try dating another fighter?"

"I have." On the road, any given gym was practically man-meat banquet in the run-up to a big event. "But at the end of the day, the last thing I want to talk about after a training session is UFC gossip, or the carb content of a baked potato."

"I could see that. So what's this guy do, the one Jenna found you? Do you know?"

She tried and failed to bite back a grin. "He's a sports medicine doctor."

"Ooh la la, look at you go. That's the kind of friend we could use around here. Do me a favor and marry him."

And since Steph was practically drunk on possibility, she imagined exactly that.

THE HOT DOCTOR *was* hot. His digital profile photos proved it, and he was funny to boot, and polite, and he'd typed his Thursday-night introductory email in full sentences, with capital letters and punctuation. His name in the signature— Dylan Benedetti—was followed by an exciting parade of authoritative initials, none of which Steph could translate beyond the M.D. Barring a Bruins medical crisis, they'd be meeting at eleven-fifteen the following night, at a trendy bar only a few blocks from the gym, near Boston Common.

News of Steph's date spread instantly. Rich ribbed her non-stop through their Friday shift, proving himself a bottomless well of medical innuendo.

Patrick, the least qualified electrician ever licensed in the Commonwealth of Massachusetts, was busy testing the new security system all day. Steph found the frequency with which he peered at exposed wires and muttered, "That's weird," highly disconcerting. More disconcerting still was that he'd apparently arrived at seven, yet was still working by the time the evening sparring session was winding down. If he wasn't sandbagging to scam his boss for extra pay, he had to be plain old incompetent.

Steph and Rich were sitting on the mats, facing one another, cooling down after the evening's sparring. Their soles were pressed together, and they held hands, taking turns leaning backward to stretch the other's hamstrings and arms and back. The thirty or so members who'd braved the snow and ice for a chance to scrap were doing the same, more than a few looking skeptical about the exercise, or perhaps the hand-holding. Wilinski's boxer types might have power on their side, but they could stand to adopt Steph's regimen of flexibility drills. She was only too happy to torture them into better shape.

"Be careful with this fancy doctor guy," Rich warned. "One flash of that stethoscope and he'll have you disrobing before your starters even show up."

She rolled her eyes at him.

"He'll probably want to dress you in one of those paper robes and get freaky with the tongue depressors."

Steph leaned way back, reveling as Rich winced. His turn came to pull, and she let him tug her all the way forward until her arms and chest met the floor.

Rich laughed and eased her up. "That ain't natural."

They got to their feet and Steph could feel the past couple hours' exertion in her muscles. She should be exhausted to boot, but with every minute that ticked by, bringing her date closer and closer, her heart beat quicker. She'd hoped the workout would burn off the nervous energy, but nope.

Still, she was prepared. She'd taken Jenna's advice, finding herself an overpriced pair of stylish jeans and a pretty cashmere sweater. The promised snow had arrived, so heels were a non-option, but Steph had brought a pair of dressy black boots that looked good under the jeans.

"Okay!" Rich shouted to the group. "Everybody hit the

showers, stat. Steph's got a hot date and needs to make herself pretty."

A bunch of the guys taunted her with seedy whistles.

"Make it quick," Rich added. "He's a doctor."

They chided her with extra *ooooh*s before dutifully heading for the exit and locker room.

Steph looked to where The Worst Electrician Ever was messing around with the security panel. "Why is he still here?" she murmured to Rich.

"The locks aren't engaging or something. He said it'd be fixed in ten minutes."

They walked to the edge of the mats, and Steph turned on her heel and gave the workout area a quick bow, the respectful reflex ingrained by years of jujitsu. "When exactly did he say that?"

Rich made a face. "'Bout four hours ago?"

Misgiving squirmed in her middle.

Fifteen minutes later, the members had all cleared out and she and Rich exchanged an uneasy look.

"My sister's car's in the shop," Rich said. "I'm supposed to pick her up from her shift at ten-thirty."

She eyed the clock. She absolutely *had* to be out of here by eleven sharp, but that gave Patrick forty minutes to fix whatever he'd messed up. "You go ahead."

"You sure?"

She nodded.

"Right then. Good luck tonight." He gave her a clap on the shoulder and headed for the exit.

She crossed the gym to where Patrick was tinkering. "How's it coming?"

"It's coming," he said brightly, turning to beam that stupid-making handsome smile at her.

"I have to be out of here at eleven, at the *very* latest."

"No worries. I'm so close, I can taste it."

"Have you been tasting it since this afternoon?"

"Trust me."

She didn't trust him, though. Didn't trust his skills any more than she might've trusted her body in the same room as his, back in her mid-twenties.

"I have to get cleaned up," she said. "So if you have any business in the men's locker room, please refrain for the next twenty minutes."

"Nope. I'm good."

I just bet you are, she thought, eyeing his arm as he turned back to his puzzle. Good man to have on your July Fourth softball team, good to his mother and his friends, always good for a lusty tumble on a Sunday morning.

Far too good at that last one, surely.

But the instincts that had her imagining such a thing were bad, bad, bad.

Mind over body, she reminded herself. It was what let her fight through the pain and work past her limits, and if she could harness it in a ring, she could do the same in her romantic life.

"All clear?" she shouted into the men's locker room, finding it empty. She grabbed her gym bag and headed inside. She'd enter as sweaty Steph, and emerge a new woman. She'd stripped and faced dozens of opponents hell-bent on knocking her down. There was no reason she couldn't dress up and face this latest challenge...even if it had her more nervous than she'd felt in years.

Still, she liked the nerves. *Loved* the nerves.

She twisted the shower tap, and waited for the hot water that would rinse away the old Steph for the rest of the night.

PATRICK STARED AT the diagram in his hand, then the panel on the wall.

Diagram, panel. Panel, diagram.

Man, he should sue whatever jerk had marketed this product. Easy five-step installation his ass.

He'd guessed this job would take him two hours—cut the holes, fit the boxes, marry the wiring, home in time for the Bruins' opening faceoff. Now it was past ten. And he couldn't just call it a day and deal with it in the morning—that'd mean leaving the gym unlocked all night.

Maybe it wasn't the security system. Maybe it was the building's wiring. But he'd checked those connections a thousand times…maybe a thousand and one was the magic number? He opened the metal door in the corner.

Ridiculous. This former factory probably predated electricity, and the basement's wiring looked like spaghetti, each generation of improvements layered on top of the previous. Patrick was a pretty awful electrician, to be sure—he was a carpenter by trade, bumbling through this contract out of economic necessity—but this was just *unfair*. Getting this system to work was like grafting bat wings onto an elephant then commanding it to fly.

"C'mon," he goaded, tinkering with one of the connections.

The lights flickered and he quickly turned the screw the other way, making a mental note to not touch that one again.

A moment later Steph came marching out of the locker room. There was a towel fisted between her breasts, though she still had her bra on and her hair was dry.

"What was that?"

Pretty ballsy of her, considering she was alone in this basement with a strange man. Or maybe not. Patrick pictured the flurry of bad-ass kung fu moves she might lay on him if he pretended to rush her. Better not try it.

"Just a little flicker. Nothing to worry about." Worrying never helped anything, anyhow.

Her gaze went to the clock mounted above the boxing ring. "You're nearly done, right?"

"Oh yeah. I'm sure I'll have it fixed in five." Mentally, he crossed his fingers. She didn't strike him as a woman who liked to be kept waiting. "Your nose looks better," he offered. Not as swollen as yesterday. And she seemed less intent on murdering him, if only by a fraction.

"Just be quick, please."

"I probably connected the wrong wire or something simple like that. The electrics in this place are ancient. Half the wiring's still knob and tube, and all the old labels have flaked off." He smiled hopefully, but she headed back toward the locker room.

Too bad he'd bashed her in the face and tripped her. He'd totally have asked her out if he didn't suspect she hated him. Although maybe if he fixed this stupid system, she'd change her mind about him. Yeah. Save the day at the very last minute, and she'd forget all about the injuries.

He turned back to the panel, spurred by this mission. Where could he invite her to go? What did lady-ninjas enjoy doing, off the clock? He could just let her pick and go along for the ride. *He'd overheard the fighter guys teasing her about a blind date. Those never panned out. She was as good as single.* And she was really pretty and different, and it was sexy, the way she looked at him, all…skeptical. He'd gone out with a couple girls since his divorce, but he'd found the process frustrating. Women were so polite on first dates, then you got your hopes up and called the next day, only to find out they weren't into you…?

A woman like this one wouldn't bother with the cheery agreeableness. She'd tell him point-blank that walking along the beach in the dead of winter was a terrible idea, unlike that woman he'd met the other week. Alicia? Alyssa? Didn't matter now. She'd dodged his call asking about a second date, texting a tardy, *Not into it. Sorry.*

Damn. You spent six years off the market and when you rejoined the dating world, everything was different. You had to treat your Facebook page like a police report and learn how to text. You had to find yourself on Google and try to guess what a stranger would make of the results.

Patrick shook his head, singling out the last connection still to test. He swapped its wire with another, holding his breath.

With a *bleep,* the security panel's Satanic little red light turned…green!

"Yes, you beautiful bastard." Just tighten that screw and—

The lights went out with a crackle. "Uh oh."

He loosened the screw. Nothing.

Steph's voice came through the darkness. "Hello?"

"Yeah," he called. He headed toward the locker room, guided by the scant glow of the streetlights coming through the high windows. "I'm still here."

"What happened to the lights?"

"I'm not exactly sure. But good news! The locks are working."

"That's great, but it's ten degrees out and I need to dry my hair. Could you get the power back on? I'm in a hurry, here."

"Hang on."

He fumbled for his Maglite, illuminating the space between them. Steph was dressed in her towel again, her long wet hair plastered to her neck and shoulders. Quite without meaning to, he let the beam drift down to her chest.

"Can I help you *find* something?" she demanded.

He hoisted his gaze to her face, along with the beam.

"Oh Jesus." Her hands flew up to block the blinding light, an elbow clutching the towel in place.

He aimed the flashlight at the ground. "Sorry." He sure wound up using that word a lot around her. "My bad. And sorry about, you know. Your chest. It's… That wasn't my fault. That was just biology. You know. Because you're in a towel. Sorry."

He wished she'd just go and get dressed. His attention was being dragged down, down, from her chin to her neck to her collarbone, her freckled skin dotted with water, hair dripping. He hauled his eyes back up. "Maybe you should... you know. Put some clothes on?"

"I'm not done with my shower. Maybe *you* should fix whatever you broke so I can get on with what I need to."

Again, his gaze dropped to her breasts, utterly by accident.

She gaped at him. "Oh my *God.*" And with a mighty glare, she flashed him.

Patrick blinked, barely registering the glimpse of full-frontal female.

She reknotted her towel. "Curiosity satisfied? I'm a natural redhead. I'm sure you were wondering. Now *fix. This.*"

Never mind the wiring he'd botched—Patrick was more worried about the stuff short-circuiting in his head. "Uh..."

"Listen, Patrick McFlan O'Shanahan or whatever your last name is—"

"It's Doherty."

She tossed her arms heavenward. "Of course! Of course it is."

Never piss off a redhead, his dad's voice echoed. Too late. "You realize you're the most Irish-looking thing that ever was, right?"

"I've got a date in forty-five minutes. I haven't had an excuse to smell nice in over six months, let alone one that involves a hot doctor, and I am *not* missing this. So whatever you messed up, fix it."

"What's the magic word?"

"Do you want to stay employed?"

Right. Close enough. He could let the rudeness slide in light of him invading her privacy, clocking her in the face, tripping her, trapping her at work late, ogling her, blinding her, and endangering her chances with some fancy doctor.

"It's probably just a tripped fuse or something." Or something. Patrick's electrical chops were suspect under the best of circumstances. He'd been certified by a buddy he'd graduated high school with, and landed this contract through his cousin. So no, Patrick wasn't the most qualified guy for the gig, but hey—a job was a job. And he goddamn needed this one.

"If for some reason I *couldn't* fix it…"

Her brow rose.

"What about what's his name? The manager? He said he lives upstairs. He could at least come down and maybe take over, so you can go on your—"

"He's in California 'til Tuesday."

"Oh."

"We're probably the only people in the entire building."

"Hang on. Let me check the fuse box—could be a totally simple solution."

Her eyes were blazing hot, burning his back as he crossed to the panel in the far corner. He stole a backward glance as he swung the metal door open. She hadn't budged. She was just standing there, glaring daggers at him, arms locked over her chest—her modest but perfectly feminine chest. He fiddled with the connections by the shaky beam of the flashlight, but nothing. Not so much as a flicker. Frowning his apology, he returned to the seething statue formerly known as…Sara? No, that wasn't it.

"I'll just run up to my truck and grab a book. It's got, like, every electrical issue there is and how to fix it."

Her narrowed eyes said he'd better be *literally* running.

"Hang on." He jogged for the front exit. He fairly slammed bodily into one of the double doors—the bar depressed but the lock didn't budge. "Ow. Damn." He shook his aching wrist. He gave the other side a fruitless push. "It's fine," he called as he hurried toward the rear emergency exit. "Just some glitch with the new system."

He grabbed the handle and twisted it down—nothing. Twisted it up, another big heap of nothing. "Oh come *on*."

"No," she said, striding over by the light of her phone and elbowing him aside. "No, no, no." She grasped the handle, twisting and tugging and pushing and pulling in every possible combination. "Oh, you are *kidding* me." She checked her screen, her sigh rattling with frustration and despair.

"Let me just disarm the system." He ran for the front.

"No need to rush," she called. "There's no way I'm making it on time now."

But there was also no way Patrick was giving her any more reasons to think he was useless. If he was going to screw all this up, the least he could do was be speedy about it.

He flipped the security system's plastic panel up, but something was wrong. No red light, but no green light, either. The screen was black. That shouldn't be. It was supposed to connect to the same power supply the emergency lights ran off—

What emergency lights? he had to wonder. They hadn't come on when he'd blown the main ones. "Oh crap."

"No," she said, stalking over. "No 'oh crap.' Why 'oh crap'?"

"Listen, I'm sorry, but I can't fix this. I don't even know what I did."

She blinked at him. "But that's your job. You're the guy we'd call to come and *fix this*."

"If I could get at my book, maybe I'd stand a chance. But this thing's as dead as the lights." He tapped the security console with his flashlight.

She rubbed her temples. "You are a *terrible* electrician."

"I know. But I'm an amazing carpenter."

She gaped. "Then what are you doing here, botching a job you're not even qualified for?"

Keeping a roof over my head? "Don't worry, I'm licensed."

"Somehow that doesn't comfort me." She wandered a few paces away, face lit by her phone's screen. She put it to her ear, staring at Patrick as it dialed.

"Hello, Dylan…? Yes, it is. Um, I've been better. I'm really sorry about this, but I have to miss our date. I'm sorry it's so last minute, but I'm trapped at work…No, I'm *actually* trapped at work. We're having a new security system installed and the electrician's managed to lock us in with no power…Yes, I'm looking at him right now. I'll tell him." She put the phone to her shoulder and told Patrick, "He says you owe him a date."

"I'm not really into doctors."

She spoke to her phone. "I'm so sorry about this. Want to touch base when you're back in town…? Okay. Great."

Patrick whispered loudly, *"Tell him I said you look great naked, and he's totally missing out."*

For a breath she beamed poison at him, then returned to her call. "No, thank you, really. I was looking forward to tonight…What are the chances, right? Yeah, you, too. Good night." She hung up looking defeated, but calmer.

"Won't it be cute," Patrick said, "when you guys get married, and you get to tell this story during the toast?"

It didn't look as though *cute* were quite the word she'd have picked to describe this situation. "You have a half hour to get us out of here before I call the fire department." She turned to head back to the locker room.

"Wait, wait, wait." He tailed her, stumbling over a gym mat. "Don't do that."

She wheeled around. "Why on earth not? We're trapped in a building with no power, with no working exits and no way to fix it. How is this *not* fire department–worthy?"

"Because whatever comes after that is probably going to cost an arm and a leg—getting some emergency electrician out here, or whatever they'd do. And whatever comes after that will definitely get me fired."

"No offense, but you *ought* to be fired."

"Listen…" He dredged his memory for her name, but the image of her naked body seemed to have crowded it out. "Sorry—what's your name again?"

"Steph."

"Right, right. Listen, Steph, I've got a mortgage to pay and—" The flashlight beam had dropped to her chest again. He raised it enough to register the murder in her eyes. "Sorry. I can't lose this job."

"You can't *perform* this job." She snatched the flashlight from him, illuminating her chin ghost-story style, the more seductive parts of her mercifully lost in the shadows.

"Let me call my cousin. He owns the company and he's a *way* better electrician than me. I'll get him to help me figure out what I messed up, and maybe you, me and him are the only people who'll ever need to know about any of this…?" He let her see how desperate he felt, gave her the shifty hound-dog eyebrows and everything.

"Do you have any concept of how unprofessional this is?"

He ignored the temptation to suggest that flashing strange men in your place of work wasn't exactly Employee of the Year material, either. "I do."

"If there was a fire, we would *die* in here. And given how great my evening's going so far, that's the obvious next step."

"Please. Let me call my cousin, and if he can't walk me through it…" What, then? He didn't have the first clue, but he really *couldn't* lose this job. If he did, his house would go next, an idea too awful to contemplate. "Lemme call him, okay? Please, Steph?"

Her shoulders dropped. "Fine. I'm going to finish my

shower, and if you still don't have a clue by the time I'm dressed, I *will* call 9-1-1. I'm not sleeping in here all night."

"Great. I'll need my flashlight back, though."

She slapped it onto his palm, hard enough to sting, and relit her phone, illuminating her way into the locker room.

3

STEPH TOWELED OFF by her phone's scant glow and pulled
on her date clothes.

Any second now, she chanted in her head. Any second
now, the lights would come back on. *Please,* let them come
back on. She didn't want to spend the night here. Her evening had sucked hard enough already.

But she also didn't want to get Patrick fired. Technically
he probably deserved it, but he reminded her too much of
her younger brother, Tim. Sweet guy, but so clueless. She'd
be angry to hear about anybody getting Tim fired for screw-
ing something up—which he probably did every single day
at the auto shop where he worked—and it made the idea
of doing the same to Patrick feel gross. Though she would
firmly suggest he look into a third vocation.

She found him in the back corner of the gym before the
open fuse box, talking on his phone, flashlight gripped between his arm and ribs.

"No," he was saying, "it doesn't *have* one. This thing's
practically made of mammoth tusks. Half of it's still K
and T."

Steph tugged the flashlight free, aiming it at the panel
as he poked and fussed.

"Thanks," he mouthed.

The fuse box was a massive thing, with rows and rows of toggle switches and several dead, frayed wires leading nowhere. This building was easily over a hundred years old, and not well maintained. Perhaps this would be a tricky puzzle for even a decent electrician to solve. Maybe he *was* a decent electrician. Maybe his evening was proving even more frustrating than hers. She felt embarrassed for bitching him out.

"Yeah," he said. "I think so. Hang on." He set his phone down and pulled on a pair of gloves from his tool belt. Steph stepped away a pace, watching his back flex as he messed with something or other. She could see the shapes of his lats and traps and the swell of his deltoid, and wondered how he'd gotten those. She'd always had a weakness for a man with a nice back. She pondered what he might look like, doing push-ups with his shirt off—

Suddenly, a miracle.

She gasped as the overhead lights flickered to life with buzzes and ticks. Patrick whooped and picked up his phone. "You hear that? You are a *lifesaver.* I owe you. Again. Okay, go back to sleep. Oh—who won tonight? Nice. Later, man."

He turned to Steph, beaming and incredulous. Smiling this way, he made her forget how annoying he was in light of how *handsome* he was. Nothing flashy, just an honest sort of face, but that smile lit him up. It lit her up, too, in ways she'd sworn she was done feeling toward guys like Patrick Doherty.

"Okay," he said. "Now all I have to do is make sure the security system's working and we can get the hell out of here."

They walked to the front of the gym.

"Green light!" he said as the panel came into view. But his smile drooped as they got closer. Not green—yellow.

"What does yellow mean?" Steph asked, pushing on the bar of the door. Still locked.

"I dunno."

They peered at the little digital screen. Custom settings lost. Enter access PIN to reactivate default settings.

"That's okay," Patrick said. "It'll only take a minute to re-program the hours." He crouched for the manual, finding the label printed with the device's serial number and code.

"Four nine four, zero two two…" He hit Enter. The light turned red. PIN not recognized.

"Hmm." He entered the digits again. PIN not recognized. 5 incorrect PINs will result in system lockdown. Two chances blown.

"Let me see." Steph gave it a try, but he hadn't misread the numbers. PIN not recognized. 5 incorrect PINs will result in system lockdown. "What the hell?"

"It worked earlier. Maybe there's some other code in here, for this situation…" He flipped through the booklet. "Or I could look up troubleshooting tips on my phone."

Dear God, the so-called expert they'd hired was going to *Google* his way out of this? Wilinski's really did need all the help it could get.

"This is still an improvement," he said.

"How?"

"We've got power again. And lucky for you, I got that new flat-screen all wired up. Why don't you watch a movie or something? I'm sure I'll figure this out in no time."

Steph wished she believed him, but nothing he'd yet done had instilled her with even the *tiniest* speck of confidence. "Fine."

She dried her hair in the locker room then grabbed a sports drink from the fridge in the office, jotting it on the lengthy I.O.U. list Mercer kept taped to the wall.

In the screening room there was a shelf lined with VHS tapes and DVDs—old boxing matches and MMA footage, plus a nice library of fight flicks. She picked *The Karate Kid,* her favorite from kindergarten. The movie had probably shaped the entire course of her life. She hit Play. Two recliners sat side by side, and she plopped into one with a weary huff.

She was supposed to be at a bar, nursing a vodka and tonic and hitting it off with Dr. Dylan. Yet here she was, drinking Powerade at work well after closing time. Story of her life. The past couple years, she'd often lamented feeling trapped in the gym. This was just *sick*—the first week of her fight retirement and here she was, *literally* trapped in one.

She was just nodding off, mouthing along with the movie dialogue, when a knock on the doorframe jerked her wide awake.

Patrick was smiling in a way she didn't trust one bit.

"So?"

"Yeah, so…"

She groaned. "Seriously?"

"I got nothing, here. If I punch in one more PIN and it doesn't work, the cops get called."

"Can you call the security company?"

"I did. They're sending a guy out."

She relaxed back in her chair.

"He'll have a service PIN that'll disarm the system from the outside. But he has to do it in person—it requires a code *and* a key. He can't just give me the digits."

"Oh well."

"But the guy on call is over in Chicopee, so…"

"*What?* Oh come *on.* That's two hours away!"

"Sorry." Patrick unbuckled his tool belt, set it aside and sank heavily into the other recliner with a wailing of springs. "This time it really isn't my fault."

Good God, two more hours…? But what was the alternative? Call 9-1-1 and get the door busted in, probably wind up stuck here answering questions and filling out police forms, with both the manager and owner out of town… Plus if this really *wasn't* Patrick's fault, it'd be a shame to drop him in trouble over whatever fees they might get charged if the fire department had to bail them out. She could appreciate that as lousy as her evening was turning out, at least she wasn't worried about whether or not she'd still have a job come morning.

"Okay," she said with a mighty shrug of surrender. This night was just destined to suck. Might as well embrace it. "I guess we'll just have to wait it out."

He turned in his chair, leaning his arm along the headrest. "I appreciate it. And I'm sorry."

"You're still a terrible electrician," she reminded him. "But maybe this could have happened to anyone, given how old the wiring must be. And *maybe* it's the company's fault the system's not working. Though it's weird both those things should have gone wrong in one night. To one man."

"Luck of the Irish."

"You would know, Patrick Doherty."

"Maybe it's fate that we got trapped here together."

She raised an eyebrow.

"I'm single," he said casually. "You're single, for as long as I can keep you out of that hot doctor's clutches…"

"Please don't hit on me. This evening has been enough of an ordeal already. Let me just watch my movie and take a nap, and we'll both pray the security guy can fix all this in like, two seconds. Then we'll never speak of it again."

She shut her eyes, but Patrick didn't make it even a full minute before interrupting her snooze. "So, your job…"

She sighed, meeting his eyes. "What about my job?"

"So are you like a pro-lady-wrestler, or…"

If looks could kill, hers would've punched straight through his heart and out the other side. "I'm a jujitsu instructor."

"That's what that's called, all that rolling around in a karate outfit you were doing the other day? Joo jitzoo?"

Lordy. At least he hadn't called them pajamas, she supposed. "It's called a *gi*."

"But it's basically wrestling, right?"

"Brazilian jujitsu evolved from judo, and yeah, it's a grappling-based martial art. But I don't get greased up in a sequined bra and booty shorts and body-slam other women."

"What do you do?"

"Have you never seen cage fighting?"

"Not really."

That would never do. She sat up straight, chair back snapping to attention.

This wasn't how Steph had planned on spending her evening, but she might as well make good use of the time by educating yet another person on what MMA was all about. She went to the shelf, finding a VHS of one of the best pro events there'd ever been from way back in the sport's more lawless days. Patrick had to help her, switching the video input to the VCR.

"See?" he asked, crouching beside her, switching cables, close enough for her to catch the annoyingly pleasant scent of his skin. "I'm not *completely* useless."

Steph hit Play and they returned to their seats. "Now pay attention and I'll show you exactly how *un*-like pro-wrestling this is."

"Yes, ma'am."

"Do you ever watch boxing?"

"I don't follow it, but yeah, I've seen a few matches."

"Kickboxing?"

"Does that Van Damme movie count?"

"Nearly. Anyhow, MMA is way more like boxing than pro-wrestling. For starters, it's *real*."

The event coverage started up and she fast-forwarded, skipping over a particularly bloody preliminary match.

"Whoa," Patrick muttered.

She stopped when the tape reached the main event. It was an epic fight—nonstop action, the perfect mix of stand-up and grappling, a million exciting reversals and near-submissions.

"So, wait," Patrick said halfway through the first round.

She turned, finding his lips pursed, brow furrowed adorably.

"Yes?"

"So you actually do this?"

"I do. Or I did. I'm just a trainer now, so I won't be doing much more than sparring. I'm getting old for it." Some fighters could stay professionally viable all the way to forty, but Steph wasn't destined to be one of them. She could feel the sport taking its toll in her joints, and her post-match aches and pains lingered far longer than they had when she was twenty.

"But you got hit in the face and stuff?"

"I did. Plenty."

Patrick's blue eyes studied her. "It doesn't show."

"Well. Thank you."

"Except for your nose, but that's my fault."

She waited for him to get predictably obnoxious with the topic, and ask if rolling around with women turned her on, if anybody ever had wardrobe malfunctions, if perhaps she'd like to wrestle with *him,* here and now. But after a moment's contemplation, all he said was, "Huh."

"Huh what?" She hit Pause on the remote.

"I dunno. That's cool. Can you…"

Can I what? Pin you? Come on, out with it. I've heard them all.

"So can you stop somebody from like, attacking you?"

She blinked, surprised at the question. "Not if they've

got a gun. But yeah. I fought off a mugger once. And one time I was hiking with my friend and somebody's dog attacked her, so I kicked it."

His eyes grew wide with horror. "You kicked a dog?"

"It was attacking my friend! It should have been on a leash."

"Poor dog. It was probably just protecting its owner."

"It punctured her skin!"

"Poor dog," Patrick said again, and Steph realized he was winding her up.

"You own a dog, don't you?" How could he not?

He frowned. "I did. I lost her in my divorce."

Divorced. So Patrick Doherty wasn't just floating through his easy life, drifting blindly from one opportunity to the next on a cloud of lovability.

"What breed?" she asked.

"Pug."

She had to laugh.

"What?"

"I dunno. You just seem like a Golden sort of guy."

"Well, I wanted a black Lab, like I grew up with. But my ex was in love with those pugs. And she was a great dog—really sweet. Just not the kind you can toss a Frisbee for on the beach."

"How old are you?"

"Thirty-five in April."

"Were you married long?"

"Almost four years. We split up the Christmas before last."

As someone currently hell-bent on finding a partner, Steph couldn't help but want to ask what had gone wrong for Patrick and his. She held her tongue.

He smiled at her, a warm and disarming gesture. "You can ask what happened. I can tell you want to."

She bit her lip. "What happened?"

"I kinda wish I knew." Leave it to poor, charming, clueless Patrick to not even know what had ended his marriage.

"I was really happy. I loved my wife, I loved our home. I loved how we spent our free time. I was just checking my watch, thinking we'd probably socked away enough money to start talking about the whole baby thing."

"But she hadn't been thinking the same?"

He shook his head. "Not the way I was. She told me, 'I want to be able to stop working when I become a mother, but that's never going to happen, is it?' She's a corporate accountant—she made *way* more money than me. I said hey, I'd be happy to only take weekend work and do the stay-at-home-dad thing. But that wasn't cutting it for her. *I* wasn't cutting it."

"Ouch."

"All this resentment came pouring out of her like a volcano. All this anger I'd never even realized she felt toward me. I just…" He shrugged, looking utterly lost. "My own wife thought I was a failure, and I didn't even have the first clue. I'd thought we were *fine*. It was so weird, like we'd been living in these two completely separate realities."

Steph's heart hurt for him. How often had her dad beat himself up with those same feelings of provider inadequacy?

"You said you're really a carpenter?"

He nodded. "I'm a great carpenter. Craftsman-type stuff, ornate trim and cabinetry. I moved to the North Shore thinking there'd be tons of work, restoring all those amazing old colonials." His eyes lit up, simply talking about it. "And at first, there *was* tons of work. Everyone was buying and flipping fixer-uppers during the boom. I was turning jobs down left and right, cherry-picking the coolest ones. That's how things were when I met my wife."

"Then the real-estate bubble burst?"

"Yeah. Now I'm lucky if I get even one job a month, fixing somebody's deck for a quarter of what I might charge doing the custom stuff I'm really good at."

"That's too bad."

"Trust me, I wouldn't be here now, wrecking your day, if I didn't need the money. My mortgage was steep to begin with. Take away my ex's income and it's a bear, even after the refinancing."

"Can you not sell it?"

His gaze dropped to the armrest, where he rubbed at the worn leather with his big fingertips. "Maybe I could. At a loss, though. And I've put so much work into that place… it'd break my heart. It's a great old house—not huge, but right on the beach, in Newburyport. I've put *years* of my life into fixing it up, thinking it was where my kids would grow up. And I mean, they still could. Who knows? But not if I can't keep up with the payments."

She nodded, sadness deepening. She could appreciate that—pouring your heart and soul and sweat into a purpose for months and months, only for it to come to naught. She'd trained for and lost enough matches in her career to understand that heartbreak perfectly.

"That sucks," was all she could think to say. She reached over and gave his forearm a commiserating pat, same as she would have if one of her brothers had broken some bad news. But this touch felt nothing like she'd expected. The contact *zing*ed straight up her fingers and arm, dropping through her middle like a gulp of hot chocolate, warmth sinking right into her toes. Oh no.

She snatched her hand away, clasping her fingers. No no no. She was *not* entertaining this attraction for a *second*.

This was all wrong.

It was probably pushing 1:00 a.m. She might've been kissed by Dr. Dylan Benedetti already, had this evening gone to plan. Yet here she was, locked at work with the embodiment of every guy she'd ever dated and sworn to put behind her…and he'd just *zing*ed her. It *had* to be some kind of test.

But she could admit Patrick wasn't quite like all those exes. He was in his thirties for one, with a marriage already under his belt. Lovable cloddishness aside, he was a man, not a *guy*. He'd suffered more disappointment and shouldered more responsibility than she'd have guessed. And these extra dimensions only made her sexual attraction feel all the more charged and unwieldy. And reckless.

Steph hit Play. They watched the tape through to the end of the match, and she stole sidelong glances, smirking at the way Patrick winced.

She shut it off. "So that's MMA."

"That's barbaric."

"The rules have gotten stricter since that event. No knees to the face once a guy's on the ground, that kind of thing."

"And that's what you do? Or did?"

She nodded.

"On TV?"

"Not always, but a few times."

"It must pay well."

She shrugged. "At the top, yeah."

"Were you at the top?"

"No. But it's what I love. I made enough to make it worth it."

"Until now."

She stretched, and let her arms flop along the back of the recliner, feeling the hour. "I'll be thirty in a couple weeks. My body doesn't bounce back the way it used to, and I'm tired of all the traveling. I'm ready to settle down."

"With a hot doctor."

She smiled. "Wouldn't hurt."

"Blind date, right? Who hooked you guys up?"

Her cheeks warmed. "The matchmaking agency upstairs."

"Oh. I hadn't thought of trying that…I've had crappy luck doing the bar scene again, and the online stuff intimidates me. I have no idea what to say to make myself sound interesting. Going through an actual service must be expensive though."

"Yeah, it is."

"Figured. Better keep trying my luck at the local dive, one drink at a time. Though if this thing with the hot doctor doesn't work out…" Patrick began.

This again? "Yes?"

"Would *you* want to maybe go out with me sometime?"

She shook her head. "No, thank you."

His face fell. "Is it because I'm recently divorced? Should I not be telling women that?"

"No, you're just not my type." *Not anymore. Never again.*

"That's too bad. But I guess I can see how I might not be, if doctors are more your scene." Sadness drew his brows together, a look that said he felt he should've guessed as much—that he should've known from the circumstances of his divorce that he wasn't cutting it these days as romantic material. Poor man. Steph's heart twisted anew.

"Plus I did sort of wreck your entire day," he added.

She managed a smile. "Not my *entire* day." Only the most exciting part, the chance she'd been dreaming about since she'd decided to leave the road behind. But still. "This isn't the worst thing that's ever happened to me. And you haven't made me bleed tonight, which is an improvement." She laughed suddenly.

"What?"

"Hold up your hands."

He did, and she pretended to count his fingers. "Wow, all ten. So you're only a danger to others."

He smiled, some pink rising in his cheeks. "I've been jumpy all week, trying to dumb-luck my way through this contract. I'm not nearly this much of a klutz when I'm doing my own thing."

"I'm sure."

"Plus the time with the extension cord—that was because you made me nervous."

"Did I?"

"The first time I met you, I whacked you in the face. Plus you know...you've got sort of crazy eyes."

"Crazy eyes?"

"Yeah, you've got them now."

She sighed, knowing he was right. Her mom called that look Penny's War Face. Her annoyance was about as covert as a swinging mace.

"Plus you were all sweaty," Patrick added, a bit too innocently.

"That's kind of my job."

"I know, but you smell really good, all sweaty."

She shot him a doubtful look.

"Like sex," he concluded with a nervous, guilty grin.

"Oh Lord."

"It's true. Made my brain short-circuit. So really, the tripping thing was mainly your fault."

"Please don't flirt with me."

"Like that really good, sloppy sex, the kind you have when you stumble home half-drunk after the Fourth of July fireworks?" He grinned.

Damn, she knew that sex, too. Knew the exciting weight of a fun, fearless, sexy guy like Patrick tumbling across tangled covers with her. She knew that sex, punctuated with smiles and swears and dares and laughter. With playful, whapping pillows and the sort of deep, resonant orgasms that only came when you felt free and happy with a guy, partners in that awesome silliness. A man like Patrick could provide between the sheets. But it wasn't enough. Not at thirty.

You're not thirty yet, an evil voice in her head whispered. *Maybe one last little taste of what you're saying goodbye to?*

But a date was not one last little taste. So what exactly was she thinking of? She eyed his mouth. His shoulder and biceps and those big fingers. His damnable smile.

"I'm real easy," Patrick said. "As a date, I mean. *This* could be our date, if you want."

"This?"

"Sure. We've got movies. And two single people. Done!"

Steph rolled her eyes at him, but Patrick was already leaving his recliner. He killed the overhead fluorescents and shut the door partway, effectively dimming the lights.

"Oh, no."

"What movie?" he asked, kneeling before the DVDs.

"This isn't a date."

"It may as well be. We've got time to kill." He flipped through the spines. "Man, there's a lot of Hebrew movies in here."

"I believe that's Thai you're looking at."

"Oh, right."

"Though speaking of which…" She left her chair and crouched beside him in front of the shelf, finding what she was after.

"What is it?" Patrick asked.

"You'll like it. It's one of the most irresistible fight flicks ever made."

She popped it in the DVD tray as Patrick switched the video input. She relaxed in her chair. Patrick went to the side of his, pushing their armrests flush. She shot him a look as he took his seat.

"What? It's a date."

"So you seem to think." But she settled back in her chair, rendered involuntarily giddy by the flirtation. It'd been ages since a guy had tried making anything resembling a move on Steph, and she'd forgotten how nice it felt.

The opening scene of *Ong Bak* started.

"Why are those guys all covered in mud?" Patrick whispered. "Is this a dirty movie?"

"Shush. Just watch." Perhaps the subtitles would demand their full attention and cool the ridiculous, misplaced warmth Steph felt creeping between them. She had to be imagining that. Couldn't be his body heat—there was still a good six-inch buffer between their arms. It couldn't be infatuation, either—not this soon, not from this clumsy a wooing. Then again, it *had* been a while... Her defenses were weak.

They watched the movie for a time. Or in Steph's case, she pretended to watch the movie. Though her eyes were on the screen, her awareness was purely on Patrick. On that tangible heat. On the mistake her body begged her to make, tussling with her resolve.

Then perhaps twenty minutes in, Patrick laid his forearm across the divide and took her hand. She blinked, too upended to say anything, to pull away.

Oh dear, his fingers were warm. A carpenter's fingers, big and rough and capable. He beamed her a look, a sort of sheepish admission of guilt, a naughty boy wondering how long he might get away with something.

She didn't dare squeeze back. Or rub his palm with her thumb. But she couldn't seem to extract herself, either. For minutes on end, he held her hand, until their palms grew warm and damp and intimate. Until the movie's epic market chase scene began, and then she was in trouble. One of the most exuberantly, joyously choreographed sequences ever filmed, and she was a goner. When Tony Jaa hurtled through the barbed wire, she clutched Patrick's fingers tight.

She relaxed her hand immediately, turning in time to

catch him smiling, eyes on the action. But every time something amazing went down—*squeeze, squeeze, squeeze.* They weren't even at first base, but her body was already broadcasting her excitement, no matter if it was inspired by the movie. Or rather, *please, please, please* let him assume it was inspired by the movie.

There was a creak as Patrick planted his elbow into the armrest, leaning close. She should have been wording a brush-off, but the shape of his clenched arm distracted her.

One last time. One last taste of this flavor of man, a palate cleanser before the next course arrives, the next phase begins.

His mouth was close, posing its silent question. Steph was torn between two answers, two choices, two selves— her past and her future.

His lips quirked to one side, tense with unspoken words. "What?"

"We've both had pretty shitty days," he murmured.

True. She held her tongue.

"Personally, kissing you would improve mine," he concluded.

She had to laugh. "I've been nothing but snappy with you this week."

"And I've been nothing but dangerous to you."

He meant bodily harm, but Steph found another angle. Dangerous to her plans, her focus; tempting and foolish as a drink when she ought to be one-hundred-percent focused on an impending match. "When is your contract done?" she asked.

"The second the security system's a go. Theoretically, this afternoon at three o'clock."

So he wouldn't be coming back. This really *could* be a one-time thing, no awkward run-ins. She'd likely never bump into Patrick again.

She leaned in. He held her fingers tightly and brought his mouth down to meet hers.

Oh God, it positively *crackled* through her, this kiss.

Patrick might've been the worst electrician on the planet, but this hot bolt zapping through her veins was something else. It'd been a few months since she'd made out with a guy, but this excitement went far beyond the merciful ending of a drought. That damned chemistry, like she'd felt with some of her exes. Rough fingers making her nerves prickle, that honest scent of Patrick's any-guy soap. Why did blue-collar men have to dismantle her common sense this way, and make bad decisions feel so frigging *right?*

Whatever. This was a farewell kiss—one last dance with her past before she moved on, once and for all. Goodbye to all the fun she'd had with the guys back home. *Thanks for the memories, I'll think of you fondly.*

His fingers slipped from between hers, curling against her palm—even that simplest friction drew the breath from her lungs. His other hand came around to cup her shoulder, its warm weight drawing her close, leaving her reeling. His full lips were by turns firm and soft, toying with hers. He cocked his head and she obeyed the unspoken command, letting him in. Just the softest sweep of his tongue to start, a tease that strung a hot, taut ribbon of desire from her mouth to the tips of her toes. More tongue—a slick intrusion, sensual but with the slightest bossy edge. A shiver crept in alongside the maddening heat. Steph was a physical woman. She liked a lover who could get demanding in bed. Liked that intimate battle, and the rough press of a man's fingertips at her hips or back or butt. Patrick's touch told her, *I can give you that.*

The hand on her shoulder slid up, thumb pressed along her throat, fingertips tickling the nape of her neck. That hint of domination. Steph spent so much time fighting to maintain physical control in the ring that getting pushed around by a guy held a wicked appeal. When it came to sex, she happily shed her power alongside her clothes.

She had to rewrite a few of her assumptions about Patrick, kissing him now. His tongue promised precision, his strong hands possession. He was no galumphing puppy when the lights went down, she realized. Nothing in this kiss promised anything less than complete mastery.

The more they kissed, the fuzzier her brain grew. The more they kissed, the closer their bodies crept, each of them mashed against their armrests, legs cocked to the sides, aching to tangle. He held her neck with both hands, then one slid down her shoulder and arm to cup her bent knee.

Do it, her body urged.

Don't you dare, her head countered, and she wasn't sure which of them the warning was meant for.

Strong fingers slipped into the crease behind her knee. His kisses grew distracted as he debated, and she waited. Then it came—the softest tug.

She ignored it. A deeper kiss, a firmer pull. She offered the slimmest surrender, letting him draw her calf over the armrest. His mouth turned hungrier as he stroked her leg from her ankle to her knee. The next time he tugged, it was more an order than a request, and that distinction alone crowded out the last of her common sense.

Steph obeyed.

She let him urge her bodily across the divide, until her knees were planted on either side of his hips. Goddamn him. Goddamn these thick thighs between her slim ones, and the hardness of the muscles she felt flexing there. She braced her hands on the back of the recliner as they found their way with the kissing. Those big, warm hands were on her waist, begging. She ignored his pleas, locking her legs and keeping their crotches firmly separated. She was helpless enough from the eagerness of his touch. If she felt any more evidence of his excitement, she'd be a goner.

His plaintive hands grew antsy. They slipped lower and he stopped asking, and started dictating. He held her hips tight, and drew them firmly down to meet his.

She gulped back a groan. He was stiff. He was *ready,* and he could be rough, if a woman asked for that. She felt it in his grip. His fingers made promises, echoed by the hard length of his arousal, pressed to her mound. She could reach between them and find out if his cock matched the rest of his big body. Her palm found his shoulder, his hard arm, firm chest. *Grab my hand,* she beamed. *Don't just let me do it*—make *me do it.*

She could hear his excitement in the pitch of his breath and the rumble of his low, soft moans. Those sounds fit his body, that deep baritone echoing through his frame. She could imagine it all now—broad chest, strong shoulders, roped arms bracketed against Steph's sides in a nest of twisted sheets—

Careful. But Patrick's advances were anything but careful. His fingers curled around her wrist. He didn't force her hand, but he would, soon enough.

He murmured, "I haven't felt this in ages."

Shit, that voice. Those hot, needy words. They landed like the meanest hook, sending her better judgment staggering. *You haven't felt what?* A woman's willing body, or something far more dangerous—a connection like this one, crackling hot, lethal as lightning.

His kiss grew deeper, hungrier. It invited reckless decisions and wild sex, sweet soreness come morning and—

His phone jingled and buzzed and Steph shot up like she'd been Tasered.

She stared around the dim room. How long had they been kissing? Ten minutes? An hour? The movie was nearing its climax and she fumbled back into her own chair.

Patrick looked drunk, eyes unfocused. He cleared his throat and dug his cell from his hip pocket.

"Hello? Hey, John… Excellent, hang on." He looked to Steph. "What's the code to get into the foyer?"

She waded through the sex-fog clouding her brain. "One zero two two, eight two."

He relayed the digits. "That got it? Excellent." He pushed the footrest down, standing. "Head to the end of the hall—the door to the gym's at the bottom of the stairs. Yup, I'll stay on."

The strain of arousal lingered in his voice, but he covered the more incriminating evidence handily, strapping on his tool belt around his hips.

The lights of the gym flooded the lounge as Patrick pulled the door open, heading for the exit, voice fading. "Thanks so much for coming, man. I sure hope they're paying you time and a half…"

Steph blew out a long breath, feeling drunk. She tidied her hair and pressed her palms to her cheeks, trying to banish the heat there. What had she done?

Nothing. You kissed an electrician. At work, granted, and on the night you were supposed to be kissing a doctor. Just the latest in a long string of pleasurable collisions with good ol' local boys. Harmless.

She switched off the TV, hauled Patrick's recliner back to where it should be and grabbed her empty bottle. Leave no trace of this final encounter. She wouldn't even remember it a week from now.

Then as she headed for the door, she cast a final glance at the two innocent chairs, probably still warm from their overheated bodies. *Bad, bad, bad,* she thought as she pulled the door shut.

She licked her tender lips, still flushed from Patrick's demands.

Bad, bad, bad, and *way* too good.

4

STEPH HAD TO WAIT until the following Wednesday for her date with the hot doctor.

She'd held her breath all weekend, positive he wouldn't call to reschedule.... On Monday evening she'd begun to think her chance was blown, and had even gone so far as to compose a casual email to feel him out. Just as she'd been agonizing over whether to sign it "Sincerely," or "Talk to you soon," or plain old "Steph," her phone had buzzed. And five minutes of painless small-talk later, her date was back on!

"It was fate," she told Rich on Wednesday morning, when he arrived for the lunchtime rush. He'd nearly perished of laughter when she'd told him and Mercer about the accidental lock-in with the now infamous Electrician From Hell. Naturally, she omitted the bit of the story where they wound up crossing second base.

She held a hand target for Rich to whack as he warmed up for the kickboxing session. "But at least this way," she said, interrupted by a *whap*, "I'm out at two, there's no Bruins game, it's not snowing, my nose is back to normal... And I can go home and shower and nap before I meet him."

Whap. "Plus you upgraded from drinks to dinner," Rich huffed. *Whap.* "Where's this fancy man taking you?"

"Somewhere in the North End."

"Nice." Rich turned to the members shuffling in and stretching on the mats. "Everybody do five minutes' extra warm-up. It's frigging freezing out there." He turned back to Steph. "Plus this way he can upgrade *you,* if dinner goes well."

She frowned. "Upgrade me?"

"Oh sure. Pass the dinner test and he'll ask you if you want to *continue this conversation over a nightcap,*" Rich said unctuously, dark lashes fluttering.

"How do you know I won't be the one determining whether or not to upgrade the date?"

Whap. "I'm just saying, this'll be a good test. Unless you blow it, you'll definitely get a second venue. What're the rules, sex-wise?"

"You're as subtle as your right hook. And if you mean the Spark rules, it's no sex until the fourth date."

He goggled at her. "*Four* dates? If it's the right person, you won't even last the night."

She was inclined to agree with him, but their views on dating and sex were warped by the pressure cooker of their lifestyles. On the road, you might meet someone and the courtship *had* to be a whirlwind—you probably wouldn't be in the same city the next week.

"I'm going to do whatever Jenna tells me," she said. "She's the expert."

"What do her and Lindsey know about good decision-making?" *Whap.* "They wound up with Merce and me."

THOUGH IT WASN'T snowing, the slush from the last storm had frozen into slick grooves on the sidewalks, so Steph stuck with her original outfit. If money weren't an object she'd have gone for it—worn the dress she'd bought that weekend,

a sexy knee-length number in a deep green that comple-
mented her hair and eyes, plus some heels, and shelled out
for cabs. But sadly, money *was* an object. As ever. Training was steady income and Wilinski's subsidized her insurance, but it wasn't exactly a high-paying position with
potential for upward promotion. She'd saved every penny
she could from her decade as a pro, and had nearly fifty
grand in the bank—but she was determined not to touch
it, short of an emergency.

After work she jogged home, took a long shower and a
nap. Her nerves kicked in the second she woke.

An hour before game time, the hot doctor's name flashed
on her phone's screen. Her stomach curdled. He was can-
celing. This date was cursed.

"Hello?"

"Hi, Steph? It's Dylan."

"Hey, how are you?"

"I'm fine—just finishing up at work. Listen…and forgive me if this is really forward. I'm out of practice at all
the dating etiquette."

"That's fine. So am I."

"You said last week you don't drive, right?"

"Not in Boston, no."

"Well, it's freezing, and if it doesn't weird you out to
give me your address, I'd love to pick you up."

"Oh." She gave it a split second's thought and decided
his chivalry would be rewarded with a view of her legs in
the new dress. And if it went terribly…she could afford to
splash out on *one* cab ride to get herself home. "That'd be
great. Thanks."

She gave Dylan her address and he promised to call
when he pulled up in forty-five minutes.

She smiled to herself as she changed into the clingy
dress, thinking of all the guys who'd picked her up for
dates back in Worcester, honking as they pulled into the

driveway; of all the guys she'd had flings with on the road, a thumping fist on her motel room door announcing their arrival. Finally, a gentleman escort. No honking. No, "Hey, a bunch of us are gonna walk over to that bar on the corner. You want in?"

She swapped accessories and clipped the tag off the long wrap sweater she'd bought to go with the dress, practiced walking in her heels, applied and removed five different lipstick shades. She sprayed herself with perfume, then panicked that it was too much and dabbed at her cleavage with a tissue. She yelped when her phone rang at two minutes to six.

"Hello?"

"It's Dylan. I'm outside—black sedan with a very nervous man in the driver's seat."

"I'll be right down." She gave herself a final look, discovered a tag still lurking in the armpit of her wrap, snipped it. She slipped into her coat in the elevator.

To her surprise, a very handsome, trim man was standing just outside the building, eyeing the street, rubbing his hands against the cold. His breath flared steam into the night air and he turned as Steph exited.

Were they supposed to shake? Hug? She waved cheesily, but Dylan came forward and took her upper arm gently and kissed her cheek.

Oh, sa-woon.

"I'm sorry, sir, but I have a date with a man in a driver's seat."

He smiled, two dimples appearing. "I realized this is probably more gentlemanly."

He led her to a luxury sedan—sleek and new but nothing too show-offy—and opened her door.

"Thanks." She sank into the leather and Dylan circled to the driver's side. With a final whoosh of frigid air, he closed them in blessed heat.

"I turned your seat-warmer on," he said, starting the engine with the push of a button. "If it's too hot, the switch is by your elbow."

"Oh, thank you." Heated seats—nice. Her last car had boasted a cassette deck and a single, broken cup holder. She took in the handsome console, illuminating her handsome date.

Black hair, dark eyes, a slender face with a sharp, interesting nose. A shadow lingered at his jaw, though she could tell he'd shaved before he left to get her. Probably with a straight razor and a fancy wooden lather brush, finished off with expensive aftershave. He wore black leather gloves with posh stitching, making the green mittens in her coat pockets seem impossibly juvenile.

"Thanks so much for the ride," she said as he made a U-turn. "You gave me the perfect rationale for wearing heels in January."

"It's no trouble at all."

"Have you been to this restaurant before?"

Dylan told her he had. As he ran through the highlights of some of the meals he'd enjoyed there, she pondered his voice. Not *high*, just a bit reedy. But it fit his slender frame. And no man was *perfect*.

Still, for just a moment she felt bossy hands hugged to her waist, heard words she'd sworn to forget. *"I haven't felt this in ages."* Her body gave a traitorous clench.

Quit it, dummy. Don't mess up the most important date of your life, getting all squeezy over an electrician you'll never see again.

This date would go well. So well in fact, there'd be several more dates, and in a couple weeks maybe she'd feel comfortable asking Dylan to come to her cousin's upcoming wedding. Kind of a heavy proposal, but her cousin Kristy had been a jerk to her growing up. They'd been in the same grade all through school, and she'd always gone out of her way to make Steph feel like a loser—for her hair and freckles, for being a late bloomer, for dating "all those dead-end townies," for having such a weird, butch job.

Of course she shouldn't care what Kristy thought of her…but wouldn't it just be *heaven,* turning up to her wedding with a specimen like Dylan Benedetti on her arm? That probably made heaven a petty place…but who cared? After years of psychological warfare, Steph—the gangly carrot-top wannabe ninja—could make an entrance. With an enviable figure and a stunner of an escort. She'd been impulsive and RSVPed *plus guest.* Please, please, please, let it be *plus hot doctor.*

"Which made me laugh," Dylan was saying. Steph had completely lost the thread.

"I'll bet," she hazarded.

"The waiter thought the guy was ordering for the whole table! I'll say that about you pro athletes—I'd kill for your metabolism."

Ah, must be some Bruins anecdote. "I bet I'll kill to have my *former* metabolism back a year from now," Steph said. "I'm already getting soft."

"Be prepared to gain five pounds tonight—I'm ordering us at least six courses."

The drive took less than ten minutes, and he dropped her in front of the restaurant and told her to go ahead and order them a bottle of wine while he trolled for a parking spot.

The restaurant was beautiful—dim and intimate, at once rustic and sophisticated. She felt pretty as she shed her coat and handed it to the hostess. Steph gave Dylan's name and was led to a table by the front windows, complete with candles and napkin rings. It was warm and she was happy to ditch her sweater. The little cleavage she possessed looked great with the dress's draped neckline.

For the wine selection, she exploited her only scrap of knowledge—that red wine went with red sauce—and picked a mid-priced Chianti whose vineyard she stood a chance at pronouncing. Dylan arrived just as the bottle did.

"This is all right?" he asked, rolling up the sleeves of his crisp gray dress shirt.

She nodded, glancing around appreciatively. "It's beautiful." The waitress handed her a splash of the wine to taste. Was this good? She didn't have the first clue. Dylan tasted his own sample.

"Lovely," he declared. "Perfect choice."

The waitress filled their glasses and left them alone with the leather-bound menus.

As it turned out, Dylan's threat of six courses wasn't idle.

Steph would've been content with the delicious bread—crusty and steaming, dipped in seasoned olive oil. But Dylan started them with calamari, then grilled zucchini, then big slices of decadent sausage with a spicy marinade, then roasted mushrooms. He made her dominate the first hour's conversation, peppering her with questions about MMA, ones that made her feel exotic and accomplished.

She groaned as they split the final mushroom. "That was amazing."

"For the main course," Dylan said, picking up his menu, "I'm leaning toward the stuffed peppers. How about you?"

"Oh God, there's a main course still to come?" She laughed, scanning the choices. "You'll have to roll me out in a wheelbarrow."

"That would be my pleasure." Oh, that smile. Goodness, he was handsome. As handsome as an actor. She hoped she looked nice enough to match him.

She settled on one of the cheaper dishes—an upscale incarnation of chicken parmesan. She guessed this was all on Dylan's dime, but if it wasn't… The wine alone would've blown her usual dining budget, and at this rate there was definitely going to be dessert.

As they relinquished the menus he leaned in, smiling that perfect smile. "You look really lovely."

"Oh, thank you."

His dimples deepened. "I like how you blush."

She grinned, knowing even the slightest embarrassment stained her red from her neck to her hair.

"You have beautiful skin," Dylan added, eyes dropping to her décolletage with appreciation, not seediness. "That color really suits you."

Damn, this man was smooth. "That color suits *you*," she countered, nodding to his collared shirt, as polished as his haircut and tidy nails.

"So enough about me. What was your childhood like?" she asked, wondering if his smoothness was the product of a privileged upbringing, or if a person really could learn to be this effortlessly urbane.

Dylan gave her the gist—he'd grown up middle-class, in New York State, and his parents were still married, both retired college professors.

"My mom taught classics and my father taught micro-biology. Didn't offer much overlap, not unless you got them talking about the Bubonic plague."

Steph smiled dryly. "Don't think you get to just gloss over the whole New York issue. Lay it on me—Giants or Jets?"

"Busted. Giants."

She sighed dramatically. "So if this goes well, things could get ugly on Sundays."

"Does the fact that I rehab your hockey players not earn me some kind of pass?"

"I suppose it should…but still. Prepare yourself."

"You said you have a brother?"

She waggled two fingers.

"Oh dear. So I'm doomed. I'm never winning your family's approval."

She blushed anew to hear him talk about something so *advanced* on the first date. Her hopes for wedding-date redemption soared. "You'll be a hard sell. But I promise I'll defend you."

They chatted through their entrées about sports, about who'd grown up with more sadistic winters, about current events, about everything but the three topics Jenna had forbidden—politics, religion and exes.

It was, without doubt, the most perfect first date ever. All that was missing to seal that distinction was the most perfect first kiss ever.

Dylan relented on dessert, and they decided to nurse the rest of the wine in its place. He handed the waitress his credit card before even requesting the check, giving Steph no chance whatsoever to help pay. She tried to open her mouth to offer to tackle the tip, but a firm and pointed look from Dylan shut her down. She smiled. She could get used to this treatment.

When the final plates were cleared, he shifted the glass candleholder to the side, and reached across the tablecloth, opening his hand in invitation. Steph swallowed nervously and curled her fingers around his, surely red as a fire hydrant from the pleasure.

"This was really great," Dylan said earnestly.

She nodded. "For me, too."

"I wish I could ask you out for a drink, but I have an early morning."

"That's fine—I'm opening the gym at six."

He grinned.

"What?"

"You have the coolest job," he said.

She laughed. "If you say so."

"I'd love to give you a lift home."

She nodded. Dinner had lasted close to three hours—Dylan was surely fine to drive. They bundled into their coats and braved the four icy blocks to his car. The cold leather upholstery shocked her thighs.

They spoke very little on the way, and she bet he was preoccupied with the same questions she was. Would they kiss? Yes, of course they'd kiss. They'd kiss and kiss and kiss and it would be as perfect as the rest of this date. But would she invite him up?

There was a free space right in front of her building— a sign. All he had to do was switch off the car and come upstairs with her.

They turned in their seats and she said, "I'm under strict orders not to invite you upstairs on the first date."

"And I'm under strict orders not to accept such an invitation."

"Jenna's probably got spies watching us right now."

"I think I'm allowed to kiss you, though," Dylan said, smiling hopefully.

Her middle fluttered. "I think you are."

He put the car in neutral and moved in.

Patrick. He flashed across her brain, unbidden—a far different man leaning across those two armrests, wanting a kiss to cap off a far different kind of date. She shoved him aside and shut her eyes.

Dylan's lips were firm…too firm, too thin. But he was nervous, surely, same as Steph. She angled her head, softened her own mouth, hoping he'd do the same. But his lips only seemed to come with that one dry, tense setting.

It wasn't a *bad* kiss, even. Just…tidy. Much too tidy.

Patrick's mouth. Patrick's soft, full lips, capable of shifting from shy to sensual to filthy at her faintest signal.

No no no. She coaxed Dylan a bit further. Maybe he was good at making out, just not this chaste kind of kissing… But when they got there, more of the same. And his tongue was too wet, unwieldy, not matching the hardness of his lips at *all*. Nothing like those smooth, dirty sweeps

Patrick had given her, the exact right balance of slick and hungry and utterly controlled, those qualities that made a woman think of nothing but sex.

Feel something, she commanded her body. Dylan was ninety-eight-percent perfect. His voice and his kisses didn't get her hot, but in light of everything else…so frigging what? *Feel something…*

And she did. She felt Patrick's hot, strong fingers at her waist, felt his rousing kisses in place of Dylan's cardboard ones. She felt the sinful weight of Patrick Doherty pushing her into a mattress, and in a heartbeat, she was wet.

But when her eyes opened and the kiss broke apart, those blue eyes were gone, that handsome face with its honest, Irish features replaced with Dylan's more angular, sophisticated one. Her date was as attractive and charming as ever…yet a man she hadn't seen in days, who she'd never see again and didn't even *want* to see again… He was the one who'd primed her body this way.

Goddamn him. Goddamn Patrick and every other version of him who'd come before and driven Steph's libido deep into this one-note rut. Dylan just intimidated her. That was why his kissing didn't resonate. She was too nervous, too wound up, wanting this so badly to be perfect.

The next time they kissed, it *would be* perfect.

"Thanks for dinner," she said. "That was the best meal I've had in…ever."

"I'm glad." He smiled, looking eager. Looking as though that kiss had been just dandy in his estimation, not awkward or strange at all. Steph's stomach soured.

That's indigestion, not intuition. Give this lovely man another chance. He's everything on your mental checklist and more. And Kristy will die of shock when you stroll into the reception hall with him on your arm.

"I um, I'm free this weekend," she said. "If you're in town."

"I could do Friday, but then I'm heading to Toronto first thing Saturday."

"I'll take it. I'm free after seven." Normally it'd take a team of horses to drag her away from sparring, but she wasn't going to lose momentum with Dylan.

"Perfect. I'll call you Friday morning to firm things up."

Eager, she thought. Like those awful, wooden kisses. *Shush. Don't wreck this.*

With a final, sexless press of lips, they said good-night.

Steph hurried inside, going over all the excellent points of her date as she rode the elevator. A zillion wonderful moments, versus one lousy kiss. This would look like a no-brainer, come morning.

She got ready for bed, spritzing her pillow with the clandestine bottle of cologne. A very Dylan-y sort of scent. She'd smell him all night and dream about their amazing courtship. She would see him Friday. She would gently transform him into a better kisser, and then he'd be perfect.

She tossed and turned.

Every time her brain quieted and sleep was nigh…

Patrick.

Her mind filled with the remembered sensation of his body pressed to hers in the lounge, the promises his tongue had made, echoed by the firm length of his cock between her thighs. She punched the pillow, releasing a puff of cologne. It smelled cloying, suddenly. She swapped the pillow with its neighbor, but the scent lingered.

After another ten minutes spent trying desperately to shift her fantasies from Patrick's body and voice to visions of future Dylan-dates, she tossed the covers aside. Curiosity dragged her to the bathroom, to the sack of toiletries she kept under the sink, filled with half-empty hotel shampoo bottles, lotion packets, shower gel. She found what she was looking for, a tiny travel bar of Lever soap, and tore the paper wrapper open. She put it to her nose and breathed deeply.

Damn it to hell, it smelled right. Somehow smelled even better than an eighty-dollar bottle of Terre d'Hermès. She flung it in the waste basket, cursing Patrick Doherty.

And an hour later, still no closer to sleep, she slunk back out of bed, retrieved the bar of soap, and set it on the adjacent pillow.

She was asleep inside a minute, wrapped in dreams of easy, wicked sex, with a highly inadvisable man.

5

STEPH WOKE the next morning with no clarity, no clue what to do about the Dylan issue.

Thankfully she had a quick consultation scheduled with Jenna during her lunch break. She mounted the stairs, side-stepping yet more construction debris in the foyer—a ladder and boxes that hadn't been there when she'd unlocked the gym at six. The Spark office was open and she knocked on the frame.

Jenna beckoned her in and wheeled over a chair.

"Lindsey's out at the moment," she said as she shut the door. "Is it okay if we chat in here? The meeting room is a mess."

"Fine by me."

Jenna sat, peering at her computer screen, opening files. "The construction should be on hold until the lunch hour's over, so this'll be fairly private."

"Minus all the guys from the gym who wander by and see me consulting with you," Steph teased, nodding to the windows that looked into the foyer.

Jenna's eyes widened. "I didn't even think of that." Before she could get up and flip the blinds, Steph dismissed her panic with a wave.

EAST GRAND FORKS CA

"Everyone knows I joined Spark. Rich saw to that."

"If you're sure…"

"Positive."

"Right. Well, welcome to your first official consultation!" Jenna folded her arms atop her desk, eyes glittering. "I know you and Dylan had to reschedule, so how did that work out?"

"We went to dinner last night. He was…perfect."

Jenna beamed. "Excellent."

"He was handsome and polite and generous, and he asked me out for tomorrow night."

"That's wonderful!"

Steph's smile faltered and Jenna spotted it with the precision of a sniper.

"It *is* wonderful, right?"

"Technically, yes."

Jenna slumped. "But?"

"But nothing, really. He's absolutely everything I want. It's just… This'll sound dumb."

"I've heard it all, trust me."

"Our good-night kiss didn't really…do it for me."

Jenna frowned. "Ah."

"But that could've just been my imagination, or my nerves, right? I definitely want to see him again, and be sure."

"Sounds wise. Was it a formal date?"

"I'd say so."

"Maybe for tomorrow, ask if you can do something more casual. More relaxed, so if it *is* nerves, maybe you won't run into that problem."

"That's a good plan." Steph leaned back in her chair, relieved to be told that maybe it hadn't been the kiss of death, that chemistry-free smooch. *Just nerves. Of course.*

"And if it doesn't work out with Dylan, I'll find you another guy," Jenna added. "That's my job, after all. But I'm so happy to hear the date went well, over all."

"Oh yeah. I wasn't even sure they made men like him anymore."

Jenna seemed to try to suppress a grin and failed, clearly putting a mental gold star on Dylan's client file.

Steph bit her lip. "Can I ask whether or not my thinking on something is way off base?"

"You can ask me anything."

"So, I have to go to this wedding in a couple weeks. My cousin's wedding."

"Okay."

"And she was horrible to me when we were growing up. So my questions are, A, is it evil to want to bring a super handsome man with me to rub in her face? And B, how many good dates do I need under my belt before I can ask a guy to come to an event like that, where he'll be meeting my family and everything?"

"Is it a big wedding?"

"Yeah, at least a hundred and fifty guests, I think."

"Well, the bigger the guest list, the less pressure on the date. If it were an intimate family gathering, I'd say that's boyfriend territory."

"Right."

"Ditto the rehearsal dinner, if you're in on that."

"I'm not."

Jenna considered a moment. "I'd say it all comes down to the guy. Some men might get over-thinky about a wedding invite from a woman they're not exclusive with. But a guy with a close family who's hoping to move forward with you that way—he might be delighted. But this *is* a capital-B Big Date. So don't ask unless you're confident that you guys might be heading toward boyfriend-girlfriend status."

"How would I know that?"

Jenna smiled. "Great question. Ideally, because one of you will ask the other, 'Would you like to be exclusive?'"

"Oh man, like, 'Do you want to go steady?' This is so middle-school."

"I know, it never stops being awkward, negotiating this stuff. But if it's the right match, it's worth all the stress of asking."

"I guess that's true."

"As for your other question," Jenna said, "about whether or not it's evil?"

"Yeah?"

"It's only evil if you're using the guy without actually having any designs on him. If you like him, I'd say the whole rubbing him in your cousin's face thing is just a happy side effect."

"Oh, good. Because I would *love* that."

"I've actually set people up on *first* dates going to one of their high-school reunions. A family wedding might be pushing it, but I'll make a note in your file in case I run across a guy who might just love that kind of over-the-top first-date adventure. When is it?"

"Two weeks from Saturday."

Jenna clicked and typed.

She had Steph tell her more about her dinner with Dylan. They strategized about what date number two should look like, deciding that Jenna would offer Dylan some low-key venue suggestions during her follow-up call with him that afternoon.

"So, how about everything else?" Jenna asked, leaning back in her chair, swapping her matchmaker hat for her neighborly, not-quite-a-boss hat. "Settling into your new place, and the new job?"

"Yeah, everything's coming together. It's a weird sensation, all this routine. But I'm happy to—"

She and Jenna shrieked in tandem at the sound of an almighty crash. They stood to find a ladder overturned in the foyer, hardware strewn from a big metal tool box.

"Oh my God. Was someone *on* that ladder?"

"No," Jenna said, and they approached the window right as the worker came jogging past. He spotted them and flashed an apologetic smile.

Steph swore.

Patrick's expression changed as he recognized her— surprise chased by some kind of pleasure, his grin turning dopey.

"Do you need help?" Jenna shouted through the glass.

He waved her offer aside, tripping over an electric drill.

"You hired *Patrick Doherty?*" Steph asked.

Jenna nodded, pantomiming through the window until Patrick gave her the thumbs-up, yes he was fine, everything was fine. "He did the electrical work downstairs. He gave me his card before he left, and I told him if he's free, I've been meaning to replace those awful fluorescents in the foyer and meeting room with track lighting. Why?"

"He's the one who busted my nose and shoved me into a pile of hammers." Hyperbole, but considering his entrance just now, not so far-fetched.

"Oh dear."

"Good luck to you with that guy." And good luck to Steph. She'd been failing brilliantly at forgetting their carnal collision in the lounge when he wasn't even around. Now, just watching his back muscles moving under his T-shirt as he crouched and gathered the spilled hardware... Damn, damn, damn.

"He was perfectly nice when I chatted with him."

"Oh, he's very nice. Just dangerous." In more ways than one. Standing here with a pane of glass between them, Steph felt that attraction bubbling up. How could she feel this for Patrick—a man who'd wooed her with the same grace with which he'd repeatedly injured her—when she hadn't felt a glimmer of it for Dylan after the dreamiest, most grown-up date of her life? Maybe she was one of those self-sabotaging women, always getting in their own way.

Nonsense. Mind over matter—if she could convince her body it was a great idea to beat people for sport, surely she could reason her way out of this ridiculous infatuation.

"Well," Jenna said, settling behind her desk. "I guess that's the end of our privacy. Did we get to talk about everything you needed to?"

"Yes, thanks."

"Let's meet on Monday, and you can catch me up on how tomorrow's date goes. Sound good?"

They agreed on a time and Jenna wished Steph luck as she headed back into the foyer.

Patrick had reorganized his tools and was halfway up the ladder with a cord coiled down his left arm. She avoided his eyes and aimed herself toward the back stairs.

"Oh, hey! Steph!"

She turned to find him fumbling to descend. "Stop, stop, stop. Don't move." The boy would break his neck if given half a chance. She strode to stand beside the ladder, scouting for any teetering objects that might seek to bonk her on the head.

"Hey," he said, smiling, resting his treacherously shapely arm along one of the rungs.

"Hi, Patrick. How are you?"

"I'm good. Are you married yet?"

"No, I am not."

"Great! Would you like to go out with me sometime?"

"You asked me that last week. After you got us locked in a gym and ruined my Friday evening. And I said no."

He frowned. "Did I really ruin it? That was my best Friday night in ages."

As much as Patrick exasperated her, he was fundamentally irresistible. A puppy, indeed. She cast the Spark office a glance, finding the matchmaker's eyes predictably glued to them. Jenna turned back to her computer, frantically fake-typing.

"Please?" Patrick asked, grinning hopefully.

"I'm already kind of seeing someone."

His face fell. "Oh." Disappointment registered for a moment, then dissipated like a rain cloud. "My loss. Is it that doctor guy?"

She nodded.

"Well, can't compete with that. But you can't fault me for asking, either. Not after...you know."

She sighed.

"You said you're *sort of* seeing him?"

"Yes, I'm dating him. We're having a second date tomorrow."

"But he's not your boyfriend?"

"Not yet, no."

"So then it's okay if I tell you I haven't been able to stop thinking about you since last weekend."

She shook her head, queasy panic rising in her middle. "Don't, please. I'm no good at this dating stuff, and you're not helping."

"Sorry. But I had a really great time. If things don't work out with the doctor guy, I'd love to take you out, for real. You know, and earn all that stuff that happened between us."

Her cheeks heated and she scanned the foyer for arriving gym members. "Thanks, but no thanks."

He nodded, looking bummed. "I guess it was just me, then. Though for what it's worth, you are an *amazing* kisser."

Her blush deepened, pure pleasure, and there was no hope of hiding it.

Patrick smirked, seeming to enjoy embarrassing her. "Thanks for ending my make-out drought, at any rate."

"Um, sure."

"When Jenny—"

"Jenna."

"When Jenna asked me to do the lights for her, I thought maybe it was fate."

"It's not, I'm sorry."

"Right. Well, good luck. I'll see you maybe, today and tomorrow."

"I'll be sure to wear a hard hat."

He gave her one last dopey smile, then began climbing his ladder. She headed for the stairs, shaking her head.

PATRICK WATCHED STEPH disappear down the gym's steps, taking a little chunk of his ego with her. Oh well. He'd tried. And at least he'd managed to make her blush one last time.

He should have known the second he'd knocked the ladder over that Steph had been nearby. She turned him into a clumsy wreck. The woman did things to him, with her hair pulled back in that bandanna, no makeup, all those freckles, those greenish eyes, even her freaking *posture*... It was way too easy to imagine her next to him, those sexy arms flexing as they worked on some project together. The smell of her sweat, and how perfect she'd look, drinking a beer on his deck, watching the waves.

Those were dumb things to contemplate, though. He didn't know her. Maybe she hated beer. She might actually hate *him*. He'd caused her an awful lot of pain and trouble, so the animosity wasn't exactly unwarranted.

He did want her, though. Bad. She'd rewired something in his head when they'd kissed, and even if she couldn't stand the sight of him, he was dying to get his hands on that body, and feel her enjoying his in return. And he hadn't wanted a woman this much since he'd been courting his ex-wife. He'd forgotten how awesome it felt, *craving* somebody. That was a positive development in itself, proof he was moving on. He'd just have to enjoy *wanting* Steph in lieu of actually having her.

Too bad the kiss hadn't affected her the same way. Maybe she was *that good* a kisser. Maybe all her make-out sessions were that mind-blowing. And she thought *he* was dangerous—she ought to be required to carry some kind of liability insurance, if that was her superpower.

The rest of the job went smoothly, and Patrick got the foyer's lights operational right on time, free to head home at three. He'd tackle the job in Jenna's office tomorrow— should be just as quick. Too bad, really. No more excuses to run into Steph. She might hate him, but seeing her made him feel so good. Like a beam of scowling, freckled sunshine.

He cleaned up the mess and gathered the materials for the next day's work, knocking on the door to the match-making place.

Jenna smiled as he entered. "All done out there?"

"You're all set. I'm afraid I scratched up your hardwood when the ladder fell, but I can smooth out the marks with some wax tomorrow."

"Sounds good."

"Okay if I add this to the mess I've already made in your back room?" He held up a spool of wire.

"Absolutely. And if possible, could you come after eleven? I've got a couple clients to meet with first thing, but after that, you can make all the noise you want."

"Works for me." He wouldn't mind sleeping in, and it wasn't as though he had any other jobs to rush off to in the afternoon...or indeed a hot date, like some people around here. His stomach knotted at the thought. At imagining Steph gifting her mysterious doctor with those mind-alerting kisses.

He bade Jenna a good afternoon and bundled up in the entryway. It was so damn cold this week. To save money, he'd been turning the thermostat down to fifty when he left the house, and he didn't relish the frosty hour of waiting for the heat to kick in when he got home. He tugged on his gloves and carried his tools to his truck, parked along the curb. The engine had been irritable since the temperatures dropped, so he sat idling as it warmed up. A woman passed, limping slightly, lugging a gym bag. Damn, he knew that butt.

He hopped out, skidding on the lumpy gray ice. "Hey, Steph!"

She turned, red eyebrows rising under a white pom-pom hat. "Oh, hey. Again."

"You need a lift?"

Her eyes shifted to his truck, narrowing with distrust.

"It's freezing out here. You're limping. And for once it's not my fault. Get in."

She stayed rooted to the spot. "I live ten minutes away."

"Perfect! I can make it three."

Her eye roll told him she hadn't meant it that way.

"C'mon. It's icy and cold and my truck's all warmed up."

"Have you been waiting for me to leave?"

"What?" He blinked, catching up to her logic. "No, no. I'm not clever enough to stalk anybody."

That seemed to melt her some, and Patrick grabbed his chance, hurrying forward and wrestling the bag from her hands, nearly making her slip. She let it go with a glare. "You're not taking no for an answer, are you?"

"Nope." He took her duffel and stashed it behind his seat, then opened the passenger side for her. She climbed in, babying one of her legs.

"What happened?" he asked as they buckled their seat belts.

"Nothing. I tweaked my hamstring."

"There's no guy who needs messing up for hurting you, then?"

She smiled drily. "I'm quite capable of messing a man up for myself, thank you."

He merged them into the beginnings of rush-hour traffic. "Where am I taking you?"

"Just over the bridge, past South Station."

"Done. How was your day?"

"Fine, I suppose. How was yours?"

"I had a job, and I got to see you, so it was pretty great."

Her steely look parried his smile.

"I seriously can't flirt with you, huh? Am I coming on too strong? I'm kinda rusty at all this."

"All this?"

"You know, talking to women. Having crushes."

She laughed quietly.

"What?"

"You really are just…right out there, aren't you?"

"I know. That's probably why I'm not having any luck dating." He slowed with the rest of the vehicles snaking through Downtown Crossing. "I'm probably supposed to keep women guessing whether I like them or not."

"That's probably what some pick-up artist would say… but as a woman attempting to learn how to date properly, I can't say I find that strategy very appealing."

"Am I appealing at all?" he asked earnestly. If any woman would give it to him straight, surely it was this one. "Or is it a complete turn-off, having a guy tell you right to your face that he's into you?"

"You don't even know me, so it's a little weird."

"No, but I want to *get* to know you."

"Don't get me wrong, it's flattering…"

He nodded. "Okay, good."

"But it's… Listen, Patrick."

Damn, his name sounded great when she said it.

"You're a perfectly sweet man. And you're very attractive—"

"Oh yeah?"

"—and you seem really honest and just like, a good guy."

"But?"

"But you're not my type. Not anymore. I've dated a dozen guys *so much* like you, and it never works out. I'm thirty next week and I need to learn how to do all this. All this adult courtship stuff that most people figure out when they're fresh out of college."

"That makes two of us."

She blew out an exasperated breath.

"So you've dated a dozen guys like me," he said, "but not *me*. Maybe I'll be lucky thirteen." He inched the truck forward, spotting the cranes across the harbor that explained the traffic's glacial pace. "I mean, you think I'm honest and nice and you're attracted to me. What else does a person need to deserve a chance?"

He turned and she met his gaze, apology in her eyes.

"What?"

"Stability," she said quietly.

"Oh. Like, financial stability?"

She nodded, attention shifting to the immobile traffic.

His heart sank. *That,* he couldn't offer. Not at the moment, maybe not for a couple more years, not until the housing market recovered or he woke up to discover he was suddenly a competent electrician.

But Steph was allowed to set her own standards, and of course he'd prefer to be well-off, if choosing were all it took. This past year had been the worst in his life. The divorce was the biggest factor, naturally, but the money anxiety was a different kind of stress, chewing away at his nerves. At his sense of security. Physical security, in the form of his home, and also the security of feeling worthy. Being man enough.

He'd never been an anxious guy until last year, but a few months back his doctor had prescribed him something to take the edge off his racing thoughts and help him sleep. He'd yet to fill the scrip. He didn't want pills. He wanted to be partnered again, not left alone to shoulder all these worries. He wanted some capable, determined woman like Steph back in his life, someone he could take turns being the strong one with, through their individual struggles.

"I'm sorry," Steph added quietly.

"Don't be. You're allowed to want whatever you want." He shot her a smile. "I was just hoping I might be it."

She returned the smile. "In a previous life, you were." She held his gaze, and it was the most open he'd yet seen her, like she'd dropped a layer of armor.

A horn blared and Patrick jumped, finding that traffic had begun moving again.

"How about this," he said, wanting to lighten the mood. "Give me your number, so if I win Powerball, I can call you."

"It's not *just* money. It's a lot of things."

"Well, if you ever change your mind, I'm giving you *my* number." They'd come to another standstill outside South Station. Patrick pulled his wallet out and fished for a business card. Steph accepted it limply.

"Or if you ever need any carpentry done," he added. "Or if you want to watch another karate movie, and give me some secondhand dating tips you pick up."

Steph smiled, the gesture weary but warm, and she tucked his card in her pocket. "Thanks."

"I'm serious, too. I lost a bunch of mutual friends in the divorce, and I can always use new ones."

"Did you grow up around here?"

"Fall River."

"That's near the Cape, right?"

"Relatively speaking. It's near the Rhode Island border."

"And the houses brought you north?"

"Yeah. The architecture on the North Shore is just…"

He sighed dreamily. "It's exactly the kind of work I love. Plus the ocean. My only two requirements. Where are you from?"

"Worcester."

"Nice."

She laughed. "If you say so."

"I apprenticed in Worcester one summer, with a cabinetmaker. There's a ton of really cool houses out there, especially those ornate old three-deckers. I wish we still built homes like those for the masses. Places with character, you know? Instead of all the cheap, soulless condo developments you can see from the highway, and those awful three-car-garage micro-mansions people shell out eight hundred grand for."

She studied him thoughtfully, but Patrick couldn't tell exactly what the scrutiny was saying.

The jam broke and they made their way across the bridge, then down a couple side streets to a block lined with tall brick buildings.

"This is me," Steph said, pointing to an awning, and Patrick parked alongside the curb. She unbuckled her seat belt. "Thank you for the lift. Sorry it took three times longer than my walk would've."

He shrugged. "But a hundred times warmer, right?"

"True."

"It was my pleasure. Thanks for the company."

She pursed her lips, eyes shifting toward her building.

"You want help getting your bag upstairs?" He was already reaching for the door handle.

"No, no."

"Oh, okay."

"But would you like to come in for a coffee?"

His brows rose right along with his hopes. "Really?"

"Just, you know. Friendly coffee."

"Yeah, sure. I'd love that." He checked the curb for No

Parking signs, but apparently his luck had flip-flopped for the better. They opened their doors and he grabbed Steph's bag. They made a run for it, breath steaming in the frigid January wind.

Her building was an old industrial number, not as swankily redone as some others in the neighborhood, but fairly modern, to judge by the state of the lobby. He saw business names in addition to individuals posted on a tenants' list beside the elevator.

"Mix of residential and commercial?"

"A bunch of the units are sanctioned as subsidized artists' lofts," she said as the doors swallowed them and she hit the button for the fifth floor. "So those are people's studios and home offices. It's a Fort Point thing."

"Ah."

"All I know is, on any given night, there are at least two opportunities for free wine and cheese on my block, if you're willing to stand around saying nice things about somebody's paintings or photos or whatever. See?" She tapped an artfully handwritten flier taped beside the button bank, advertising an open studio that night. *Free eats! Free boxed wine! BYO stemware.*

They reached Steph's floor and Patrick tailed her, watching her limping gait. "Does it hurt bad?" he asked as she unlocked her door.

"No worse than what I'm used to. I'm just babying it." She pushed in the door and reached around for a light switch.

Patrick took in her small apartment, and the street view out its one huge window. It was hip—exposed brick with funky modern fixtures, a stainless-steel kitchenette at one end, lofted bed on the other. A sofa and TV-less TV stand were all that filled a small lounging area in the middle. Though it offended Patrick's sensibilities as a restoration carpenter, he could understand the appeal...even if it saddened him to see yet another chunk of New England history sullied with modern conveniences, insulated windows with faux muntins sandwiched between the panes. He had a soft spot for drafty old houses with crooked stairways and broad, creaking floorboards. Homes with stories echoing through their arthritic old bones.

"It's cool," he offered.

"I like it. And I've been living out of motels for so long, I don't even care how tiny it is. I'm just stoked to have a kitchen."

There were cardboard boxes stacked along the wall. "Not quite moved in yet, huh?"

"No, and I'm hesitant to get comfortable—it's just a sublet. I have to clear out by March. Though I *should* unpack, just to feel like I live someplace nice, if only for a month. Maybe this weekend."

"Nah, this weekend you'll be busy eloping with a doctor."

She shot him a smirk over her shoulder and unzipped her sporty winter jacket. He followed suit, hanging his old canvas one beside it by the door.

"So I really only have coffee," Steph said, taking two mugs out of a cabinet and setting them on the granite counter. "I'm not much of a drinker."

"Works for me."

"Cream and sugar?"

"Both, thanks."

She got a pot burbling. Locking her arms over her narrow torso, she leaned back against the counter. "So."

"So?"

"I want to hear all your dating war stories."

He smiled at that, tucking his hands in his pockets. "They haven't been too bloody…mainly just confusing."

She hopped her butt onto the countertop, and for a split second Patrick imagined being allowed to take liberties with this woman again. Imagined striding over and standing between her legs, grasping her waist and tugging her thighs tightly around his hips. He'd loved the way she felt. So different, with interesting, firm contours, a body that flexed like it was extra…*alive.* But with suppler bits, too, if you knew where to find them. Womanly bits only a very lucky man got invited to enjoy.

"Confusing how?" she prompted, and he scrambled to find the thread of their conversation.

"Well…and actually, this makes you *really* refreshing. But I kept having these dates, maybe three of them in a row, where I thought we'd had such a great, easy, fun time. Then I call the woman the next day to ask her out again, and…crickets."

"Straight to voicemail?"

"Yeah. I think once I got a call back a day or two later, saying thanks but no thanks, one text, and one never got back to me at all. It was just *torture,* waiting to hear, getting my hopes up, then getting the brush-off. Or not even that."

"Ouch. That's why I'm relieved I went with such an old-school approach. On the road, amongst my peers, dating etiquette is all digital. And completely vague."

He nodded. "I think that's the way of the world now."

"It's frustrating. You get a text that's like, 'Hey, you wanna hang out?' What's that even mean? Am I supposed to shave my legs, or are we just going to watch TV with six of your buddies?"

"Right." Patrick tried not to imagine Steph lounging around in hotel rooms with a small harem of muscular fighter guys.

"At least with Spark, there are rules in place," she said.

"Like?"

"Well, everyone's vetted, of course. And you're allowed to email and text the people you're set up with, but only to confirm details like where you're meeting, and when. For anything else, you're supposed to phone."

"If a guy ignores the rules, do you report him to Jenna?"

She smiled—that sweet, rare smile devoid of all her usual guarded skepticism. "I guess I could. But I can see the temptation of chickening out and texting, too. It's so scary, calling a stranger with the hope you might wind up kissing them. I can't fault anybody for wanting to soften the blow by making it less…personal, I guess."

"I'm awful at texting. My big numb fingers hit like four keys at once, and I don't even know how to capitalize stuff or add the right punctuation. I must look illiterate. I always call, unless it's really late."

"You have numb fingers?"

"Yeah, all my fingertips." He flexed his hands. "From rasps and sanding blocks and all that."

"Oh, of course." The coffee pot bleeped. Steph hopped down to fill their mugs, then set the cream carton and a sugar box on the counter. "I have nerve damage in my right hand from fighting," she said as they stirred. "My writing's atrocious. And my shins are basically made of wood now."

He smiled, adding more sugar to his coffee. "You're so frigging interesting."

Another blush, one that made Patrick feel warm in return, like she'd snuck some Irish into their coffees. The whiskey of sexual attraction.

"What's it like, fighting people?"

She waved toward the couch and they settled at either end, with the TV stand wheeled over to serve as coffee table.

"It's like fighting, I guess." Steph pushed off her shoes and stretched her legs out between them. He followed suit, liking how their socked feet sat side by side, hers looking tiny next to his. Damn, he missed women.

"Have you ever been in a fight?" she asked.

"Not since grade school. I was always the kid being like, 'Come on guys, everybody chill out.' But I did get in a couple, just schoolyard stuff. Never lasted longer than a couple shoves."

"Well, it's great," she said, smiling. "I love it. Obviously."

"What about it?"

"Just…when else do you get a chance to be that way with someone? Your body and your skills against theirs, your mind versus their mind. You strip everything away that passes for status in modern society. It doesn't matter if you make better money, or where you come from—all that matters is how hard you try. Everyone goes in equal, and you get judged on your effort and heart, I guess. Even if you lose, as long as you fight like you mean it and give it everything, people will respect that. It's really pure that way."

"Huh."

"Plus the rush is amazing. You and this other person, in shorts and bare feet and gloves, wanting to see who's got it. I think there's something in our animal nature that craves that. We want to clash antlers and prove ourselves superior."

He made a thoughtful face. "Go on."

"That's why politics and lawsuits and sports rivalries get so heated. We aren't allowed to test ourselves physically in polite society. You fight your enemies through lawyers and like, mean Facebook comments, right? Except in sports. When we fight an opponent or tackle him on the football field, we get to connect to that need. And the audience gets to do the same, vicariously."

"Like a war with no casualties. That's how I feel when my team's playing a really crucial game."

She nodded vigorously. "I love it. Being the one actually in there, battling. It switches me into this animal mode, and all the bullshit of the day disappears for a few minutes at a time. Just like, *Me. Her. Let's see who's better.*" Color was rising along her neck to stain the tips of her ears pink, and her greenish eyes were bright and gleaming. What was that color called? Sage?

Patrick's clothes felt all tight. Her enthusiasm was turning him on as much as if she were talking about sex. "Sounds...primal." He wondered what she was like in bed, if she'd want to pull his hair or something. He wouldn't complain. "Do you hate losing?"

"Who doesn't? But I'm a good sport, if that's what you mean. I'm a decent fighter, but I'm not the best. Physically I could never *be* the best—I've got a small frame and I injure easily. Competing's more important to me than winning. And the anticipation and training and fantasizing about winning is nearly as good." She grinned. "But winning *is* awesome."

"I get pretty heated playing Scattergories," he offered.

"When I was a kid, my parents banned me from playing mini-golf. I'd get so wound up I'd have, like, a psychotic break if one of my brothers was beating me."

He laughed. "Redheads."

She rolled her eyes. "My dad and older brother are redheads, and they're impossible to rattle...well, these days. My brother was a hothead when he was younger."

Patrick glanced at the mug in his hands and realized he hadn't even sipped his coffee yet. He didn't think Steph had tasted hers, either. It wasn't caffeine that had them both lit up this way. Was it attraction for her, too, or did she really get that excited just talking about fighting? Was she remembering everything he was? The needy physicality of their encounter in that TV room at the gym, and the way it had made him feel like a man again, in the simplest, most affirming way.

If there was anything he hadn't felt in the past year, it was *wanted*. But this woman had wanted him—in her body, if not her rational, good-decision-making brain. And that was an addictive sensation. It made him crave her, lust all mixed up with gratitude and relief. She had the power to make him feel something he'd begun to worry he'd lost, or dreamed.

He studied her as she rehashed her last match, pretty face animated, breath short as she recounted the tension. A tension rose in Patrick, too, a sharp ache. He wanted those gesturing hands on his body, those lips on his skin, her legs hugged to his waist. A hundred things he knew he wasn't likely to get, not with Steph.

She smiled after a time. "I'm boring you to tears, aren't I?"

He worked hard to banish whatever glaze had come to his eyes. "What? No. Not at all. I could listen to you talk for hours about this stuff."

There were lots of things he'd happily spend hours doing with her. Tasting her mouth, exploring her body, watching her explore his in return.

She finally seemed to notice her coffee and took a sip, then stretched her neck from side to side.

"What's it like," he asked, "being so physical all day? As a job?"

"You should know. You're a carpenter."

"That's labor, with tools. Your body's your tool, I bet. Like a dancer. Like a dancer who can kick people's asses."

She shrugged. "I dunno what it's like. I've been doing it for so long, it's all I know. I can only tell you that I loved it way more than sitting through high-school algebra, wishing it was four already so I could go to judo. Everything else I do usually feels like a chore, especially if I have to just sit in one place and concentrate. I'm kind of restless."

He smiled. "I give your so-called retirement a month, tops."

"We'll see. But I know I can't take the road anymore.

I'm restless, but I'm sick of living out of suitcases, too."
She bit her lip.

"What?"

She laughed softly, turning the mug around in her hands.
"Don't tell my younger self this, but my clock's ticking."

"For a family?"

"I think so, yeah. Or just to be settled in one place, fall
in love... All that grown-up stuff."

Now they were getting somewhere. "Have you been in
love before?"

"I thought I was, when I was twenty. Close enough, for
that age. But nothing that made me think, *this guy is the
one*." She met his eyes with her green-gray ones. "You
have, though."

"Yeah...turned out I wasn't the one, in the end."

"But at least you've felt that."

"I know. And maybe in another year I'll feel grateful
for it."

"Was she your first love?"

"No. I fall in love a lot, actually," he admitted with a
guilty laugh. "I'm one of those serial-monogamist types."

She looked curious. "Really?"

"This is the longest I've been single since I started dating at like, fifteen."

"You think you're better, in a relationship?"

"No question. I need someone to do stuff for." He smiled.
"After I split with my ex, I left town for a couple weeks so
she could get her stuff organized and move out. I went to
visit my folks, and after maybe two days, my mom threatened to send me to a motel if I couldn't quit nagging her
for projects."

"You're close with your family?"

"Oh yeah. I haven't seen my sister in over a year—she's
out in Arizona—but we talk every week. We're all close. I
want what my parents have, that happy marriage, the house

everyone comes to for Thanksgiving. Actually, I thought I *did* have it, until two Christmases ago."

She pursed her lips, then reached out and rubbed his forearm. He blushed—partly from the pleasure of the touch, partly because he knew his pain was clear. Not caring if it was off the mark, he linked his fingers with hers. Steph went still, but didn't pull away.

"Your folks still married?" he asked.

She nodded. "Thirty-five years this summer."

"That's great. I really thought that'd be me, too. One marriage, in it for the long haul."

"I'm sure most people do."

He smirked. "Now I'm damaged goods."

She thumped their hands against the back of the couch. "No you're not. You're just… You're a certified, pre-owned model. Which is good. You come with some experience. And great letters of reference, I'm sure."

"What are you, then?"

"Oh God, I'm probably a banged up old rental with all the cities I've crashed in. Now I've put myself out for scrap." She began to pull her fingers from his, but Patrick squeezed them tight, not letting her go. She met his eyes uneasily.

"I want to kiss you," he murmured.

She looked down at their legs. "I can't give you what you're looking for. The long haul."

"I know that." *Just give me* some*thing. Anything that'll make me feel like a man again, just for a night, an hour, this minute.*

She gently twisted her fingers free and scooted back, hugging her knees to her chest. "I don't think I have to tell you, I'm attracted to you. But I'm sick of…encounters. Of ships passing in the night and all that."

He wanted to feel hurt, knowing things would be different if he wasn't broke. But he couldn't, not when she'd laid it all out in black and white. Not when he knew how miserable it felt, struggling as he was now. Maybe one woman in ten would come out and tell him straight-up that was why she wasn't into him. He supposed he ought to appreciate Steph's honesty, but after this year from hell, he nearly wished for an "It's not you, it's me." At least that would let him lie to himself to save his ego, and imagine it really *wasn't* him. But it always was, wasn't it?

Slapping his thighs, he got to his feet, registering the day's work and the cruelty of winter in his achy back. He felt disappointment settling into his bones. A familiar presence, these days.

"I guess I better head home."

She nodded.

"Thanks for the coffee," he added, though he still hadn't drunk a drop of it.

"Thanks for the ride." She rose. "Maybe I'll see you tomorrow, around the building."

"Maybe. If not, good luck with your doctor."

Her smile tightened and she stood by as Patrick bundled up at the door. "Stay warm."

"See ya, Steph."

6

STEPH CLOSED THE DOOR behind Patrick and leaned into the wood with a heavy sigh.

Close call.

She'd seen it in his eyes long before he'd come out and asked—an invitation. A question. A hopeful longing, wanting them to revisit that connection they'd found in the gym.

And she'd felt every bit of it, yet somehow summoned the will to not take the bait. *You have a date tomorrow night,* she'd kept chanting in her head. *You didn't give up your pro career to start planning for a future family, only to go ahead and repeat all the same mistakes from back home and on the road. You're going to do this right, the Spark way. Do everything Jenna says.*

And surely Jenna would not advise her to make out with a man so very like all the ones she was determined to leave in her rearview.

Was Patrick so very like those lovable guys? Working-class, check. Hot and fun and easy-going bordering on dolt-ish, check. Financially dubious, check.

She could guess where life with those other guys she'd gone out with would have led—to a weekly date night at the bar and grill, to a pokey house and two kids and creeping middle age, to credit-card debt. To watching the UFC on Pay-per-view and thinking, *That used to be me. How did I end up here? I wanted so much more.*

But she couldn't say exactly how she knew that Patrick would prove different. The way he spoke about houses told her he'd found his passion, not simply a trade. She'd never articulated that distinction to herself before, but it was attractive—a person who understood the difference between a job and a craft. Who cared more about doing the thing that lit them up than the thing that paid the most. It was Steph's path, after all.

She wandered to the couch, flopping onto the cushions and finding them still warm from Patrick's body. *Two people together, both doing what they love…* Only if one of them got paid well. Passion and professional satisfaction were ideal, but not necessarily realistic.

Still. *Passion.* She remembered Dylan's kisses, praying that tomorrow night she'd discover their lack of chemistry had been a trick of her nerves. Could she live without the excitement a guy like Patrick offered? Was a guy like Patrick only exciting *because* he was a bad idea?

She sat up to bring her mug to her lips, then slopped coffee down her front at the jarring din of her doorbell. "Damn." She hurried to the intercom and pushed the Talk button. "Hello?"

"It's Patrick. I think my timing belt just snapped."

Lord in heaven. *Of course it has.*

"Can I come up where it's warm while I figure out who to call?"

"Sure." She buzzed him in.

At the counter, she squeezed a paper towel around her shirt to wring out the coffee. "Beats getting whacked in the nose," she told herself. Patrick was getting appreciably less dangerous, if not much more fortunate.

He knocked a minute later and she let him in.

"I'm really sorry," he said, stripping off his gloves. "I knew I was on borrowed time with that belt. It's been squealing for a week from the temps, but I was hoping I could deal with it when I got my next check. I made it half a block and—*snap*."

"That sucks. Can it just be replaced?"

"Not sure. I'm out of my depth. I'm good for small repairs, but it might've really screwed my engine." He rubbed his face with a sigh. "I gotta call around and see if I can find a friend-of-a-friend who'll float me the repair costs until Jenna pays me."

"I could call my little brother," Steph offered, hanging up his jacket. "He's a mechanic."

"Oh yeah?"

She nodded and fetched her phone. "He's out in Worcester, but you could at least explain to him what it looks like under the hood. He could probably tell you what the damage might be."

"That'd be great."

She dialed Tim, catching him in the middle of a riot, to judge by the noise.

"Hang on!" he bellowed. "I'm testing my surround sound!"

A moment later he was back on, and she explained the situation. Thinking Patrick could use someone to hold a flashlight, she bundled up alongside him at the door. Down the hall and into the elevator, then out into the winter cold. They walked down to the corner where his truck was parked at a hasty angle.

So much for a quiet, early night in her warm apartment, likely capped off by succumbing to inappropriate thoughts about Patrick Doherty in the safety of her bed, solo.

Their breath fogged in the early darkness, and she held Patrick's Maglite while he told Tim about the truck and poked around under its hood. A familiar scene.

Steph's toes were starting to sting when Patrick sighed and said, "Well, shit. Uh huh. Yeah, I figured. But it doesn't sound like I totally effed the engine, right? Yeah, that's something... Listen, man, thanks so much for talking me through this. I'll let you get back to the game. What's the score, by the way?"

Steph pictured her little brother in his bro-cave apartment above their parents' garage, and was left momentarily homesick.

"Nice. I— Uh huh. No shit, for real? I've got a job after eleven... Are you kidding? I'd give you my first born, if I had one. That'd be amazing."

Steph shot him a questioning look, but he wasn't paying attention.

"Awesome. Nine it is. I will, thanks. Lemme give you my number."

A minute later Patrick hung up and grinned at her. "Your brother's going to come out and take a look for me tomorrow."

"All the way from Worcester?"

He dropped the hood. "He said it's his day off, and he owes you for something to do with your windshield?"

Ah, yes. The slap shot that had sent a street hockey ball through her first car's rear window nearly a decade ago. "About time."

"So the only issue is how I'll get back here in the morning."

"Oh."

"There's trains to Newburyport from North station. But I dunno how long it takes, or if I could get back here early enough tomorrow morning..."

"Yes," she sighed. "You can sleep on my couch."

He beamed in the streetlight. "Really?"

"Sure." She got them moving toward her building. "It'd be cruel to send you home when your truck's right here.

Especially since this might not have happened if you hadn't given me a lift. But I have to be at work by noon."

"Me, too. Hey, that's great."

She held the door for him. "I've shared rooms with some real weirdos over the course of my career. I'm sure I can handle putting an electrician up for the night."

Back in her apartment, Steph woke up her laptop and they ordered calzones. "Ninety minutes' wait," she said. "I guess we're not the only ones who feel like delivery tonight."

"I'm in no rush," Patrick said. "Got no place to go, and no way to get there."

As they settled on the couch, she smiled at him. "You must be cursed."

"Why?"

"Every time I turn around, another mishap's befallen you. You're like a misfortune magnet."

He smiled, a shy, sweet little grin. "How do you know it's not *good* luck? Look where I get to spend the night."

Her heart gave a flutter, one she'd do well to ignore. She suddenly wished she had a TV so there'd be something to hold their attention aside from this relentless attraction. Her expression must have mimicked a different kind of misgiving, as Patrick frowned.

"Sorry," he said. "I'll knock it off—all the flirting. It's probably not cool, now that you're stuck with me all night."

She didn't confirm or deny. Let him think that was what intimidated her, and not the sheer *force* of what his proximity did to her body.

This time tomorrow, she might be at dinner with Dylan again. Sitting across a table at a beautiful restaurant, with the most urbane man she'd ever kissed. But would she feel *this?* Would there be this pleasant queasiness filling her belly with nerves and hope? Would she feel this heat brewing just a bit lower—this hot, antsy curiosity? She knew she wouldn't. She had a tendency to fall hard and fast for guys, lustful crushes that ignited like fireworks, and accordingly fizzled with matching speed.

No more fireworks, she'd promised herself. You couldn't warm yourself by them, or kindle them, or shed any real light on your own needs. Bright flashes of pure excitement, but then what? Just smoke drifting across the grass, just memories.

Just one last show, that mischievous voice whispered. One more blazing, crackling, sparkling finale before she went home for good, to snuggle up by the dependable flames of a serious relationship.

You fed yourself that lie once already. Too tacky, anyhow. Not fair to Dylan, and definitely not fair to Patrick. He knew the score and he wanted her anyway, but she understood now, he needed more from a woman, deep down. More important still, he *deserved* it. He deserved a lot of things, her thanks among them.

"Your flirting's been nice," she told him, and met those blue eyes. "You've made me feel really…I dunno. Attractive, I guess. Which is odd, since I'm always a sweaty mess when I see you."

"I like how you look."

"I know you do."

He smiled, guilty. "Oops. I'm flirting again."

And I'm enjoying it far too much. Patrick Doherty, sleeping in her tiny apartment… Thank God she didn't have any alcohol in the house. Why did it feel so warm in here, anyhow?

"I ought to shower," she said, standing. Escaping. "Sorry I don't have a TV or stereo yet. Feel free to check your email or whatever," she added, pointing to her laptop.

He nodded, semi-listening by the look of it. His eyes were moving over her in a curious, distracted way, though she couldn't guess what he was finding so alluring—she was dressed in a coffee-stained thermal top and lined winter track pants. Not exactly the standard-issue seduction uniform.

"You look very…*interested*," she told him. "Don't you even think about trying to join me in the shower."

He blinked, lucidity returning. "What? Jeez, what kind of a creep am I coming off as?"

"Not one who'd likely try that, but I figured I'd warn you, just in case."

"Don't worry—you haven't left me any room for doubt about…you know. Us. Ever happening again."

"Okay. Good." As nice as being flirted with felt… "Just want to make sure nothing's ambiguous."

"Nope, clear as a bell."

She offered a tight smile, then rummaged for clean clothes and shut herself in the bathroom. She studied her reflection as the water heated. She looked all…intense. Not quite the crazy-eyes Patrick had accused her of having last week, but something. Like a cat, acutely aware of a mouse in the room. Crazy *sex*-eyes. Worst poker face ever. She could tell Patrick with her words all night long that she wasn't interested in messing around with him again, but her eyes and complexion would always give away her body's true intentions.

She showered and dressed in lounge pants and a camisole and button-up sweater, rendering herself as shapeless as possible. Deodorant, but no perfume. Good. Then she wrecked the anti-seduction somewhat by putting on mascara for no reason whatsoever. She twirled her damp hair into a bun and shut off the fan and lights.

Patrick had her laptop open on his legs, watching the news by the sound of it. He cast her a quick glance and smile and she went to toss her dirty clothes in the hamper. She studied him from behind, his head and shoulders silhouetted by the glow of *The Daily Show*. How easy it'd be, to date Patrick. How familiar. How comforting, physically; how stressful, fiscally. How like déjà vu.

He laughed.

It rang in her body like a gong—a rich, resonant sound that hummed through her nerve endings, fingers, the very ends of her hair. Pheromones she could understand, or a certain man having the exact sort of face that melted a certain woman's heart. But a *laugh*. She'd never been turned on by somebody's laugh before.

She joined him on the couch and he set the computer on the TV stand so they could both watch, backing it up to the beginning. Each time he chuckled, another brick of her resistance crumbled away.

It'd feel so good to simply sling her legs across his lap, feel him toying with her toes or rubbing her calves. Last week she'd only had designs on his body, but here she was, fantasizing boyfriend-girlfriend scenarios.

Patrick Doherty...you're far more dangerous than I ever suspected that day you hit me in the face with a door.

If he tried to make another move on her tonight...

She didn't know what she'd do.

Before she'd been held back by what Dylan would think of her, should he somehow find out that she'd messed around with another man between dates. Before, she'd cared. But the voice of her stubborn, BS-proof self was getting louder the more obvious her attraction to Patrick became, and her new, Jenna-coached self was fading to a shadow of abstract, nagging *should*s.

Her stubborn self said, *It's none of Dylan's business who I mess around with. He bought me an expensive dinner, but that doesn't give him dibs on my hands or mouth or any other part of my body.*

Why, if she found out Dylan was messing around with another woman right now... Well, it'd sting, in a knee-jerk, ego-slap way, but come on. They were both actively playing the field. She couldn't rightfully call foul. And what was good for the gander better goddamn be good for the goose. She'd muscled her way through enough double-standard sexist bullshit in the fight world. There was no way she'd be making room for it in her personal life, no matter what dating etiquette might have to say about it.

When she was out with Dylan, she'd play by Jenna's rules, she decided. She was representing Spark on those dates. But Jenna hadn't sourced Patrick for her. And it was up to Steph to choose between mandates and instinct. And she'd never cared much for being told what to do.

She pulled off her socks, arranged a couple pillows behind her, and laid back with her calves flopped across Patrick's lap. He eyed her, not doing anything at first. Then he leaned forward to angle the laptop so she could keep watching, and curled his big hands around one of her ankles.

She smiled to herself. It'd been ages since she'd been this way with a guy. Familiar. Intimacy as natural and easy as breathing.

She'd lounged around in hotel rooms and fighters' apartments with casual boyfriends on the road, but those hookups hadn't felt like this. There'd been an edge to them, a mutual and mischievous opportunism dictated by everyone's transience, everyone's complete focus on the fight. Those flings had offered a release and escape from the stress of the physical grind, but not this ease.

Patrick made her feel as she hadn't in ages, not since she was eighteen, nineteen, twenty. A time before all the traveling, when hanging out with a guy this way held the promise of something real. *Does he like me? I think I like him. Maybe this could be something.* On the road all you got was, *He seems like a decent guy. His body's insane. This'll hold me until the match is over.*

Patrick's fingertips rubbed her shin through her pajama pants, the contact so subtle, so sweet…yet it made her blood quicken, rousing that restless sensation in her belly. She watched his face, knowing he wasn't taking in the show anymore—he hadn't laughed since she'd put her legs on him. He was practically holding his breath, no doubt dying to know if this was an invitation or some cruel tease.

She pulled her feet back enough to rest her heels in the valley between his thighs—nowhere near his crotch, but the message was plain, the line crossed. His gaze moved to hers and he swallowed. With a tiny smile, she nodded.

He looked to his hands. He slipped one inside the hem at her ankle, rubbing her bare skin. His thighs tensed, and his expression changed. No one showed their excitement quite as nakedly as Patrick. She could see it in the way his lips parted and how heavy his lids looked, his entire person radiating hot distraction, as though summer had come to his body.

He met her eyes and swallowed. "You just torturing me, or did you actually change your mind?"

"I changed my mind."

"How come?"

She smiled goofily, and gave him the short answer. "The way you laugh, I think." Drawing her legs away, she sat up, edging closer. Goddamn, his body was exciting. Funny how she spent her workdays rolling around with all kinds of men, and some gorgeously built ones at that, yet none of them did what Patrick could. None of them got her hot like this, simply sitting on her couch, looking all big and cozy and capable.

She rubbed his shoulder, his arm. Memorized his stubble and the shape of his lips, and finally the color of his eyes.

As his fingertips found her jaw, those bluest of eyes closed. He cupped her face and their lips met, the contact sparking in a way a deeper kiss with another man hadn't even come close to. There was an elemental *rightness* to the way their faces fit, the way his skin smelled, something that didn't come along every day—or every year, for that matter. To let it pass them by would be unnatural. Cruel.

She took their kiss further, tasting him. The fingers cradling her jaw tensed, their possessiveness sizzling against her skin. He felt it, too. She could tell from the way he held her, how his breaths had turned harsh and labored. This rare connection he opened in her...she did the same to him, and feeling this wanted... It felt nearly as good as the wanting itself.

They kissed for ages, two antsy bodies wriggling closer, needing more contact, wherever it could be found. She clutched his sweater; he freed her damp hair, tangling his fingers in it.

He moaned between kisses. Such an open display of excitement, when Steph had grown used to masking her most primitive reactions, lest an opponent spot a weakness. She'd do anything to keep hearing those sounds. Those hungry, helpless groans and grunts. And she could imagine other sounds...ragged orders in his deep voice, rising murmurs of *"Yes"* and *"Please"* as she brought him closer to—

"Steph." It was a whisper that demanded no reply. Just her name, needing to be heard, a plea or admonishment or an expression of disbelieving awe. Instinct told her, *Touch him. Run your palm down his belly and discover how hard he is from wanting you.*

But she didn't. She didn't even get the chance, as Patrick made the move for her.

That strong hand on hers—not forcing, but not begging, either. Leading. He pressed her palm between his legs with a gasp, chased immediately by his withdrawal. "Sorry."

She dismissed the apology with a slow stroke, telling him she wanted this, too. And that she wanted him this way—eager and impolite. After a breath, his warm palm covered her hand again, following its motions, then urging them.

She'd been with too many guys who did this—grabbed a woman's hand and put it where they wanted it, eager animals unwilling to wait for gratification. She liked a pushy guy, once sex was underway and consent was implicit, but resented being rushed. It felt utterly different with Patrick. There was desperation in his touch, not merely impatience.

He broke away, peeling the sweater over his head. Steph did the same, and they didn't stop there—in a minute flat she was down to her panties and bra, Patrick to his shorts and undershirt. Steph's tiny apartment felt like a sauna, the bitter January cold merely an illusion.

She clasped him again, rewarded with that warm palm on her hand. He draped the other arm behind her shoulders, a hot, firm weight that hinted at how it'd be to have him on top of her.

She could feel him now—really *feel* him, with only the thin cotton of his boxers in the way. Steph wasn't a size-ist, but she had to admit, with his thick length wrapped in her fist, there was something to be said for a big man. Maybe it didn't make any difference in a guy's physical prowess, but psychologically… Yeah, it was exciting. She explored him with long strokes, loving the way he responded, fingers shaking faintly, breaths stilted by tiny grunts.

Her touch had him helpless and she took the opportunity to explore him in the ways she'd been fantasizing about. She leaned in close and put her lips to his throat. She wanted to feel his pulse thrumming, smell his skin and hair. She kissed his ear and he shivered. She kissed his neck and felt his moan vibrating through both their bodies. Normally she liked being the dominated one, with a lover, but the power she felt in coaxing his reactions was thrilling, too.

"You feel good," she murmured.

The hand holding hers went still, distraction furrowing his brow.

She kissed his shoulder. "You okay?"

For Your Romance Reading Pleasure...

FREE!

We'll send you 2 books and 2 gifts
ABSOLUTELY FREE
just for completing our Reader's Survey!

YOURS FREE!

We'll send you two fabulous surprise gifts
absolutely FREE, just for trying our
Harlequin® Blaze™ books!

Visit us at:
www.ReaderService.com

YOUR READER'S SURVEY
"THANK YOU" FREE GIFTS INCLUDE:
- ▶ 2 Harlequin® Blaze™ books
- ▶ 2 lovely surprise gifts

▶ **DETACH AND MAIL CARD TODAY!** ▶

PLEASE FILL IN THE CIRCLES COMPLETELY TO RESPOND

1) What type of fiction books do you enjoy reading? (Check all that apply)
- ○ Suspense/Thrillers
- ○ Action/Adventure
- ○ Modern-day Romances
- ○ Historical Romance
- ○ Humour
- ○ Paranormal Romance

2) What attracted you most to the last fiction book you purchased on impulse?
- ○ The Title
- ○ The Cover
- ○ The Author
- ○ The Story

3) What is usually the greatest influencer when you <u>plan</u> to buy a book?
- ○ Advertising
- ○ Referral
- ○ Book Review

4) How often do you access the internet?
- ○ Daily ○ Weekly ○ Monthly ○ Rarely or never.

5) How many NEW paperback fiction novels have you purchased in the past 3 months?
- ○ 0 - 2
- ○ 3 - 6
- ○ 7 or more

YES! I have completed the Reader's Survey. Please send me the 2 FREE books and 2 FREE gifts (gifts are worth about $10) for which I qualify. I understand that I am under no obligation to purchase any books, as explained on the back of this card.

150/350 HDL F5AT

FIRST NAME	LAST NAME

ADDRESS

APT.#	CITY

STATE/PROV.	ZIP/POSTAL CODE

Offer limited to one per household and not applicable to series that subscriber is currently receiving.
Your Privacy—The Harlequin® Reader Service is committed to protecting your privacy. Our Privacy Policy is available online at www.ReaderService.com or upon request from the Harlequin Reader Service. We make a portion of our mailing list available to reputable third parties that offer products we believe may interest you. If you prefer that we not exchange your name with third parties, or if you wish to clarify or modify your communication preferences, please visit us at www.ReaderService.com/consumerchoice or write to us at Harlequin Reader Service Preference Service, P.O. Box 9062, Buffalo, NY 14269. Include your complete name and address.

© 2013 HARLEQUIN ENTERPRISES LIMITED
® and ™ are trademarks owned and used by the trademark owner and/or its licensee. Printed in the U.S.A.

"You said you've got nerve damage. Can you feel me, now?"

"I can. My fingers go pins-and-needles sometimes, but not constantly." She smiled at him, charmed by his concern. "What about you?" Letting his cock go, she took his hand and led it to the exposed skin above her bra cup, those hard fingertips rousing her with callused whispers. "Can you feel me?"

He cupped her with his broad palm, the gruffness of the gesture stealing her breath.

"I can feel you enough." He gave her breast a squeeze. "You're warm. And soft."

She blushed, pleased. Usually Steph only received the sorts of compliments athletic girls did—*firm, tight, fit.* She never got called *soft.* Yet that was exactly how she felt in Patrick's arms. Feminine, even a touch vulnerable. She rubbed his chest and hard belly, admiring the contrast of his size and strength, his heat.

She slipped a hand inside the bottom hem of his shirt, stroking his abdomen. "Where on earth did an out-of-work carpenter steal this body from?"

He laughed. "You're meeting me in desperate dating mode. I was a bit squishier this time last year. I was starting to worry I was the only person who'd ever see me naked again for the rest of my life, so thanks for noticing."

"Alone for the rest of your life? A handsome guy like you?"

He shrugged and kissed her nose, seeming relieved for the chance to catch his breath. "I always thought I was pretty okay-looking, but the past few months haven't exactly validated that assumption. Until tonight."

"I bet I know why you've had rotten luck," Steph said, sitting up straight and propping her elbow on the back of the couch.

"Please, clue me in."

She traced his collarbone through the cotton. "You're too nice. I bet you tell a girl you like her the second you feel it."

He blinked. "Why wouldn't I?"

"I bet you say things like, 'I think this date's going really well.'"

"Maybe. Definitely. That's bad?" He snatched her hand away, big fingers lacing with her small ones. "I'd want to be told if someone was digging *me*."

"It's sweet—it's just not really the normal way anymore. We're living in an age where the internet assaults us with variety. And possibility. People are slower to commit, I think, because they never know what the next browsing session might bring."

"That's a downer...but I don't doubt it."

"And as refreshing as your blunt approach is, a lot of women aren't used to that. There's a lot more wheedling and waiting and deciphering, these days. They might not know how to even react to a guy who's just, 'Hey, I like you.' Maybe that comes off like a game in itself."

Patrick sighed, then kissed each of her fingertips in turn.

"The only reason *I've* been so blunt with you about what I'm after," she said, "is because you set the tone to be painfully honest right away. We've stumbled into a rare bubble of crystal-clear intentions."

He grinned. "Then we better not waste it."

Arousal coursed through her at his firm touch—at the gentle push of his hands, the weight of his body as he urged her onto her back. She wrapped her legs around his waist, so excited she felt drunk. She grabbed at his hem, jerking it up to his armpits until he leaned back and stripped off the shirt for her. She raked his back with her nails as he got settled above her, and he sucked in a breath of surprise and excitement.

"Tell me if I'm going too far," he murmured.

He pressed against her lips through the two thin layers,

hard as a man could get. Insistent with promises or pleas. And she wanted exactly what he did, and had the condoms on hand to make it happen.

She begged for his motions, tugging at his hips with the rhythm she craved, ignoring her hamstring's plaintive twinge. He took her hints, stroking his erection along her seam through their underwear with long, steady thrusts. Not missing a beat, he lowered to his elbows with a surrendering sigh, and buried his face against her throat. She met each of his thrusts with a tilt of her hips, and with every crest of that hot friction, she wanted him worse. She wanted his body owning hers, wanted his voice in her ears, his skin warm and slick on hers. Wanted to lose herself against him then watch as he came undone from this same violent need. She spurred him with her hands—faster, rougher. And he gave it all.

Suddenly he moaned, pushing up on straight arms, then sitting back on his heels. His arousal was a blush along his neck and blooming at his cheeks, right to the tip of his nose and his flushed lips. He cupped himself in a still hand, catching his breath. His chest rose and fell with desperate breaths, and she craved whatever impulses he was fighting to contain. She'd been too hesitant before and now he was holding back, for her sake surely, when all she wanted was to feel a man's rough and graceless lust plundering her body.

She stroked his thighs. "I want this, if you do."

"I do…" He laughed, then cleared his throat. "I want this so much, I need to stop a minute, before I lose myself."

"Oh." She had to bite back a grin. So it was a wholly different breed of control he was struggling for.

He pulled away, urging her to sit up with him. He held her face as they kissed, those deep, wet strokes that roused her as she'd thought only more explicit contact could. The kind of contact she was dying for, frankly. His bare cock in her fist, or her mouth. A bossy hand at the back of her head, orders murmured in that deep voice. She shivered at the thought.

"Get on my lap," he muttered against her lips.

More a wish than a command, but it excited her all the same. She straddled him, welcoming the hard heat of his arousal against her own. Could he feel how ready he'd made her? Could he smell it? Was it driving him as crazy as it was her?

He laughed softly, the sound making her light-headed. He eased her back an inch or so and slipped his hand between their middles. "I'm too close again," he said with a smile. And in place of his cock, he offered the edge of his hand for her pleasure. His thumb traced the length of her lips as she moved, and with just the thin cotton of her panties between them, there'd be no mistaking how wet she'd become, how hard and swollen her clit had grown. He kissed her deeply, a new sort of kiss. It was rough and hungry, and when his tongue was done tasting her, he caught her lower lip in his teeth. He made a wondrous noise, caught somewhere between a growl and a chuckle.

He let her go, gaze moving all over her face. "Jesus, Steph. You—"

BRRRRZZZZZ.

She yelped at the doorbell.

Crap—the calzones. She fumbled from Patrick's lap, staggered to the intercom and buzzed the delivery guy in. Patrick was in no fit state to open the door.

"Hide your shame," she told him, tossing a throw pillow at his lap then scrambling into her lounge pants and camisole. She fanned her chest with her hand, willing the telltale red splotches to go away.

A knock, and she opened the door a crack. "Hi," she said, smiling at the middle-aged delivery guy. He looked annoyed, and rightly so—she should have rushed down and met him in the foyer, instead of making him navigate the elevator and corridors.

"Two calzones?" He cast a skeptical glance at her unseasonable ensemble.

"Yup!" She said it far too brightly, and signed the receipt against the wall as he slid the boxes from their insulated sleeve. She wondered if he could see shirtless Patrick behind her, pillow clutched condemningly to his lap.

"Sorry to make you come all the way up. I forgot I even placed the order."

"So I gathered."

She tipped him outrageously and he immediately cheered.

"Enjoy your evening," he said with a smirk, swapping the boxes for the slip and pen.

"Thank you. Try to stay warm."

"Try to stay dressed," he countered loudly, already halfway down the hall.

She closed the door and took a moment to shut her eyes and wallow in humiliation. When she opened them again, she found Patrick sprawled across the couch in silent hysterics, tears streaming down his reddened cheeks.

"Yes, very funny."

He wheezed and turned over, burying his face in the upholstery and thumping the armrest with his fist.

She tossed the boxes on the counter and jumped on him, straddling his butt and giving his back a good smack. He wrestled himself around beneath her, face contorted with the agony of uncontrollable amusement. She studied him until his desperate, silent laughter petered into gasps, then little stilted huffs. He wiped the tears from his eyes with a final sigh.

She planted her palms on his chest and leaned forward to glare at him. Damn, it was nice to be this way with a man again—ridiculous and playful, and physical in a way she knew he could handle. Roughhousing like kids. Except way better, because there was sex to be had.

Beneath her, Patrick was shifting back into primitive mode. She felt his cock stiffening against her inner thigh, and the amusement on his face had morphed into a different kind of helplessness.

She peeled her camisole away and sent it fluttering to the floor.

"On top of me," she ordered.

"I'm still close."

"Use your hand."

She lay back when he made room, welcoming him above her, between her legs.

"I like how bossy you are," Patrick said with a smile. He braced himself on one arm and slipped his other hand between her thighs.

The contact made her gasp—the tease of his strong fingers through her panties.

"Move like you're…you know."

Another smile, then his face became set. He stroked her with his fingertips, and moved his hips as he might if they were having actual sex, the fronts of his hard thighs brushing the insides of hers. Steph's imagination sketched in the details, imagining it was his pumping penetration giving her this pleasure. Before long he deepened the illusion, slipping his hand inside her underwear. She bucked at the feeling, at the shock of how primed he'd made her. His fingers slipped against her, but it was the look on his face that excited her most. Awe. And hunger.

"Is this good?" he asked.

Steph nodded. She was past the point of giving orders, eager to be at the mercy of this man, feeling like he was in charge of her pleasure. Like he was in charge, period.

"You can be kind of dirty," she told him.

"Like how?"

She smirked at him. "You show me."

He looked stymied for a breath, then determination firmed his features. Against her folds, she felt his fingers stiffen, uniting as a single force to trace her lips. She shivered. He slipped two inside her, added a third. He worked them in slowly, and as his touch got bolder, the pad of his palm brushed her clit each time he slid his fingers deep.

Your hips, she wanted to beg. *Move your hips again.* She tensed her thighs around them, and he felt the spurring. He began to thrust softly, as much as he could without interfering with the efforts of his talented hand.

It was plenty. All she needed was the flex of his belly, the penetration, and she was getting close. With those fingers slipping in and out, with that strained look on his face, she could imagine everything—imagine an even more exciting intrusion, one that would have this man panting and greedy.

Rougher, she beamed to him. In time she got her wish, but it looked like a subconscious change—Patrick's expression grew darker as he pleasured her, his hips losing their rhythm and grace, his fingers' motions getting faster and gruffer. She shut her eyes and imagined his cock, owning her like this...only deeper. Thicker. Hotter in every way.

The pleasure tightened, a fist begging Patrick, *more.* He gave it. He was groaning, the sound rising with every passing moment. She wanted to touch him, hold him in her hand—know how hard he was, how hot and angry his cock must feel, being neglected this way.

Through labored breaths he asked, "Are you thinking about me?"

She opened her eyes, and the reality of him, of what he was doing, was just as arousing as the sex she'd been imagining. "Yes."

"About what? Tell me."

Tell me. Ooh. Her pleasure sharpened at the order.

"About how you'd feel. Inside me. Your cock."

He swallowed, his eyes seeming to grow dark with mischief or excitement. "You feel amazing." He slowed his strokes, making her feel each inch of his fingers as they slid in, out, in, out.

The breath left her. The cocky show was as pleasurable as the physical contact. *Touch my clit.* But she wouldn't tell him to. Being the one who got told what to do was so much more fun. "Talk to me."

"Fuck, I want you." He shut his eyes, and it looked as though his pleasure had turned to pain. But he showed no signs of stopping. His strong arm flexed with every pump he gave her, chest muscles clenching, hips thumping her thighs.

His blue eyes opened, staring down at her. "Tell me you want me, too."

"I want you. So bad." *I've got condoms. Just ask me.*

But he didn't. He kept working, kept owning her with his hand. The pleasure built each time his palm brushed her clit, but it was his voice that did her in. "I'm gonna make you come."

She reeled at the words. *Make you.*

"Tell me," he said, face set, nearly mean.

"You're going to make me come."

A smile broke through that gruff expression. He dropped lower, onto his elbow, never easing up with his laboring hand. "I can't wait. Lemme see it."

She couldn't have denied him if she'd wanted to. The orgasm ratcheted tight, tight, tight, taking her with a ferocity that arched her back and ground her head into the cushion. It was a hot, furious force, scary and quenching and holy, a dozen mismatched things, all writhing together in an angry knot. He killed the stimulation right when she needed him to, slowing his strokes until his fingers were just a warm, welcome presence inside her. She opened her eyes, panting, and found Patrick watching, his gaze reverent.

"Wow," he murmured.

She smiled. "C'mere."

He slipped his fingers from her, lowering onto both forearms so their chests brushed, and giving her just a taste of that exciting male weight atop her. She kissed his lips, running her hands over his soft hair.

"Thank you."

He smiled. "You're welcome. That was awesome."

"You have no idea." *But I'll give you a clue,* she thought, grinning to herself. "Sit back."

He left her, sitting on his heels between her legs. Steph rolled the TV stand away and moved to the floor on her knees. She slapped his thigh and he sat as she wanted, feet on the floor, legs spread wide. She tugged at his waistband and he took that order as well, stripping his shorts away. Stroking his strong legs, she made him wait, savoring the anticipation and the scene. He had a gorgeous cock, but more than his length or size or any other physical thing, it was knowing she'd done this to him—made him this hard, gotten that bead of excitement gleaming at his crown—that made her ache for it. Ache to please him. She slid her palms up his thighs, one hand clasping his hip, the other his shaft.

"Oh." His head dropped back at the contact, fingers tangling in her hair. "Please."

Hoping his demands might get gruffer if she teased him, she limited the contact to her hand to start.

"Please," he said again.

Please what?

"Suck me, Steph."

Yes, sir. She lowered her face, welcoming him between her lips.

The world became his taste, his smell, his voice rumbling in those harsh breaths as she found her pace, and the faint but sinful weight of his hands on her head, fingers in her hair.

He was too far gone for orders. The only word tumbling down from above was *"Yeah,"* a pained and excited mantra chanted to the rhythm of the pleasure she gave him. His thighs trembled. His fingers gripped and loosened erratically. And finally—

"I'm close. I'm so close."

A promise, or a warning? If it were the latter, she didn't care to heed it. She spoiled him with every last trick she knew, and told him with her lips and tongue, *Let me taste you.*

"Oh. Steph."

His hands froze. His entire body locked save his hips, which clenched with each spurt of his hot surrender. With a final, tiny moan he went slack, relaxing back against the cushions, fingers releasing her hair.

"Oh God."

She swallowed and sought his eyes, finding them closed. His handsome face was pink, lips looking swollen, his ears and the tip of his nose flushed red. Adorable. He blinked at her and smiled. "Wow."

She rose and flopped down next to him. Patrick sighed, stretching both arms along the back of the couch and staring up at the ceiling, blissed out. For a minute or more they simply breathed, coming down from the lust-high, touching each other's backs, hair, nudging one another's knees with their own. Steph broke the silence with a satisfied sigh.

"Want me to heat the calzones up? They're probably cold by now."

Patrick turned to study her, looking thoughtful as he toyed with her hair. "Let's go to your neighbor's wine-and-cheese thing."

She frowned. "Seriously?"

"Yeah. We jumped the gun just now. I know you'll never let me take you on a real date, but let's go drink some wine and look at art, like I took you someplace half-classy."

She considered it, and caved. "Okay." Why not? It was still early, and they'd need to pass the evening somehow. And even if it was lame, they wouldn't even have to leave the building to get back to her place.

She pulled on her new jeans and sweater. Patrick was stuck in his work clothes, but oh well. A man in a smart shirt was nice, but deep down she still loved a guy in his old, broken-in jeans and a tee.

He waited by the door as she found a pair of flats.

She grabbed two tumblers, per the flier's instructions, plus the calzone boxes, thinking it'd be polite to bring an offering, seeing as how there was no way in hell she could justify buying any art, not on her budget.

Patrick smiled as she flipped off the lights. In the hall, he took the boxes from her and offered his arm. She linked it with hers.

"Ready for our first official date?" he asked, his smile goofy and fond.

"I better be, considering how many bases I just dragged you across."

He grinned at that, and they headed for the elevator.

7

THEIR DATE WAS FAR TOO FUN. Far too easy.

Steph had imagined being taken to a gallery opening by some polished young man Jenna might find for her, and she'd been worried. She wasn't great at small talk and knew squat about art. But her time with Patrick at the open studio was a blast. She got a little tipsy on the boxed cabernet, and Patrick charmed everyone without even trying.

By the time they headed back to her place, she was torn between two completely different sensations—an easy, happy feeling, and a curdling dread.

Dread about the date she'd be on, this time tomorrow. Dread that maybe she didn't want what she'd thought she did… All that fancy stuff. A fancy man. Patrick was messing with her priorities, but she couldn't abandon her trajectory with Dylan just because some hot contractor was dismantling her common sense with his big hands and deep kisses.

Patrick said good-night to her at the couch. She saw that invitation in his eyes again. She saw his hope there, asking if they could maybe enjoy a repeat performance of their earlier entanglement.

But Steph was a lightweight when it came to both alcohol and sugar, and in the wake of the fun, the wine had left her strung out and punchy. That plus the voice of her better judgment let her resist the bait. The same bait that had turned too many supposedly no-strings one-night stands into friends-with-benefits imitation romances with too many guys like Patrick.

It wasn't easy, though. She could still feel those hands on her body, still hear those dark, heavy breaths against her skin. Still smell him. Still *taste* him.

But with his invitation blocked, instead of a spirited manhandling, Patrick offered a kiss on her cheek. Dutifully sweet and patient, as though he'd just walked her to her door after a trip to the malt shop, and she climbed the little ladder to her loft feeling strange and bashful and confused.

She woke the next morning still confused.

The smell of coffee had roused her and she squinted across the apartment at the kitchen. Patrick was leaning on the counter with her laptop open, watching something with the sound turned way down as the coffeemaker did its job.

"What time is it?" she asked, stretching and hoping she sounded totally casual and unfazed.

He checked her screen. "Eight twenty."

"And my brother's coming at nine?"

He nodded.

Steph clambered from the loft and dressed for work in the bathroom. Funny how she'd flashed this man the other week, but now that they'd gotten each other off, she felt weird stripping down to change in front of him. He made her vulnerable, a sensation she wasn't used to. And a sensation that made no sense, considering how utterly nonthreatening he was. Well, physically. He posed plenty of threats to her best-laid plans.

As she joined him at the counter, he handed her a mug of steaming coffee, cream already added.

"Thanks."

"Sleep well?"

She nodded, eyes on the news he was streaming. "Fine. You?"

"Your couch is a bit hard, but not bad." He paused, poorly stifling a grin.

"What?"

"Actually I slept fine. I could have lain awake all night and I wouldn't have minded. After…you know."

She shot him what she hoped was a stern look, but it dissolved almost immediately. Seeking a distraction, she sipped her coffee. Exactly the right amount of sugar. Huh.

Patrick hit the mute button on her laptop and crossed his arms over his chest, leveling her with a stare.

"Yes?"

"Can I say something?" he asked. "I can't figure out if it's tacky or pathetic. But I want to say it anyway."

She hugged her cup in both hands. "Shoot."

"I know you've got a plan in motion, for your love life or whatever. And I respect that."

"Okay."

"And I know I don't fit into it, which is fine, too. But the way we keep winding up together? Like, sex-wise?"

"Yes?"

"It's really nice. For me." His eye contact faltered, gaze dropping to her mug. "You make me feel good in a way I haven't in a really long time. And I know this might get me smacked, but I just want you to know, if you want to keep, like, hooking up until you start seeing somebody… I'd be down for that. Knowing full well you're not into me for anything serious."

Steph frowned, unsure how this announcement made her feel. Insulted that he was pretty much asking her to be his booty call—or him to be hers? Sad that such a nice man was selling himself so short? But this was Patrick, and she knew he wasn't the kind of guy who dissected what he was after. He wanted what he wanted, and could come out and name those desires.

"Right," she drawled, stalling.

"Like I said, I know it won't turn into anything more. But I really like being with you that way. And I think maybe you like me that way, too. So…"

She nodded. "I hear you. And yes, it's been really nice." Too nice, frankly. "I don't know if I'll ever take you up on that offer, but thank you. Message received."

"Cool. It's good until you find your Mr. Right. Or who knows—until I find somebody."

That final thought landed like a slap. Of course he hadn't meant it to, but the idea burned. Mess around with Patrick in some casual, mutually agreeable arrangement, all the while thinking she was the one in a position to hurt him… Then *bam!* He finds someone serious first, and she could be left just as single as before, only now short a convenient lover.

She could scream. This whole dating dance was so frigging complicated and messy and *weird*.

She mustered a smile. "We'll see."

"Great. You've got my number. And sorry if that was tacky. I just really—"

The door buzzer cut him off, and thankfully so. Steph was wound up and antsy, frustrated by how tangled everything felt. She pushed the intercom button. "Tim?"

"That's my name."

"We'll be right down."

She emptied the coffee pot into a travel mug and loaded it with sugar, and they got their coats on, finding Tim halfway down the block by Patrick's conspicuously parked truck.

He turned and offered that big-ass grin. "Heya, Pen."

"Steph," she corrected. A lost cause. She couldn't remember Tim ever calling her anything *but* Penny.

He introduced himself to Patrick, and they looked like a perfect pair in their canvas work jackets and jeans and boots.

The day was cold, but not as cruel and gusty as it had been. There was a promise of snow in the air... Maybe Steph's date with Dylan would get called off due to a blizzard. And damn it to hell, that had been a hopeful thought, hadn't it?

She stood by as Tim and Patrick got to work, offering the mug and holding the occasional tool. Inside twenty minutes, the men were joking and laughing like they'd known each other since grade school, and if this were the afternoon, Tim surely would have finished the job by suggesting he and "Pat" head to the bar and catch the game.

Mercifully, on the continuum of slip-up to catastrophe, whatever had happened to Patrick's timing belt fell on the more harmless end, and the men managed to replace it with little more hassle than a bunch of smeared grease.

After testing the engine, Tim dropped the hood and gave it an affectionate smack. "And she's good to go."

"You are a *lifesaver,* man. How much do I owe you?"

"Not much. Just the part and an hour's labor."

"And the drive," Patrick said.

"Nah, the trip's included. Sibling discount. I'll send you an I.O.U. when I get around to it—shouldn't be more than fifty, sixty bucks."

Patrick's head dropped back with relief. He took the mug from Steph and held it up in a toast, drinking deeply. "Thank you—both of you. God knows how much you've saved me on a tow."

"My pleasure, man." Tim offered his gloved hand and gave Patrick's a hearty shake.

"Oh." Patrick dug through his wallet for a business card. "If you ever have any carpentry work that needs doing, I'll give you an awesome rate."

"Gimme a few of those—I'll hand them around the auto shop."

Patrick gave Tim all the cards he had. "I better head out—I need to go in search of some hardware before I head to my job. Sorry I can't give you a ride," he said to Steph, looking legitimately bummed out.

"I'll be fine. Thanks again for the ride last night," she added, then felt her cheeks warming at the accidental double entendre.

Patrick thanked Tim one last time then climbed into his truck, pumping his fist triumphantly when it started once more. With a wave, he pulled away from the curb.

"Well done, Pen," Tim said.

Steph rounded on him. "Well done how?"

"That dating service actually works, huh? And here I thought you were wasting your money."

"Mom just can't keep her mouth shut, can she?"

He grimaced, realizing he'd just broken whatever silence vow their mom had sworn him to. He shrugged. "Whatever. He's got my blessing."

"We're just friends. He's been doing contract work at my new gym."

"You're not dating him? How come?"

"Because I've dated nothing *but* guys like him since I was seventeen. I want to try something new."

His brown eyes narrowed. "What's he doing parked outside your building, then?"

"I tweaked my hamstring and it was two degrees out. He gave me a lift. But we're *not dating.*"

"That's a waste. He'd fit in great back home."

"Marry him yourself, if you like him so much."

Tim let it drop, but it was too late—she'd already imagined introducing Patrick to her older brother Robbie and their folks, and yeah, he'd fit right in. They'd be head over heels before he even got his coat off.

Steph checked her phone. "I may as well head to work. Want to give me a lift?"

"You got it."

She ran inside for her gym bag as Tim warmed up his car, and soon they were crawling toward Chinatown through the morning traffic.

"Are you bringing a date to Kristy's wedding?" Steph asked.

"Nah. Too much pressure, wedding dates. They give women ideas. And the chick I'm seeing now is the kind who'd take those sorts of ideas *way* too seriously."

"Then I bet you she'll take *not* being invited equally seriously," Steph warned.

"I'd rather suffer a fight than a bunch of hints about what kind of engagement rings she likes."

"I really want to bring a date," Steph said wistfully. "An insanely handsome, successful date to rub in Kristy's stupid face."

Tim laughed at this regression to her ten-year-old self. "I bet you do. She was such a bitch to you when we were kids, wasn't she?"

"Unless my date tonight goes perfectly, I don't think I've got time to find someone." And something in her gut knew the date wasn't going to go perfectly. From the outside, it might *look* perfect, but on the inside... Her heart still had Patrick's big fingerprints all over it, for better or worse. Surely worse. "Here. This is my building."

Tim parked along the curb. "What about Pat?"

"Patrick." She frowned. "I think he likes me. A lot."

"How's that a bad thing?"

"And a family-wedding invite is a pretty major signal."

"So?"

"I don't want to lead him on."

"Oh." Tim put the car in Neutral. "Because you think he's not good enough for you or something?"

Patrick and Tim were cut from the same cloth, and she could appreciate how that might rub him wrong. "It's not that he's not good enough. Not at all. It's just that he's… Well, he's broke."

"And?"

She goggled at him. "And why would I sign up for that, after watching how stressful it was for Mom and Dad? It's not like I make some amazing salary and can afford to support the two of us, if it got serious. I don't want to be poor."

"That's harsh, Pen."

"Maybe, but I don't care. I'm not asking to marry a millionaire, just someone stable. I don't think it's that unreasonable a standard to have. Neither does Mom."

Tim frowned. He hero-worshipped their father, and it would hurt him to imagine his mom advising his sister not to make the same mistake she had or something to that effect. Or perhaps of any woman thinking she could do better than, say, a mechanic who lived in the apartment above his parents' garage.

"Not because she regrets what happened after Dad lost his job," Steph assured him. "Just… Why would you *choose* to struggle if you've got the choice?"

"I guess," Tim said, not sounding convinced.

"Anyhow, that's why I'm not getting serious with Patrick."

"Not getting serious?" he asked, grinning, angst forgotten. "Meaning you've already gotten *somewhere* with him."

She rolled her eyes.

"Fine, fine. Dropping it now."

Steph undid her seat belt. "Thanks for the ride. And thanks a *ton* for coming out to help. We're officially square on the windshield."

"Cool. See you soon?"

"Probably not until the wedding, but I'll be sure to make a long weekend of it. Hug Mom and Dad for me."

"You got it."

"Love you. Drive safe." She opened her door and dug her bag out of the back, and with a wave, Tim merged into the traffic.

He'd been a bit slow to mature, but he was turning into a reliable guy, if not the highest flier. Anyhow, twenty-six was the new eighteen. Give him a few more years, and he'd get there. A good, solid, hardworking guy, not unlike Patrick Doherty. And God willing, not dogged by the same crushing debt.

Warmth enveloped Steph as she headed for the gym's steps and through the foyer where Patrick had installed the track lights the day before. She glanced up, thinking they looked good. Much nicer than those old fluorescent ones. Far more flattering to any woman who might check her makeup in the little waiting area—surely Jenna's precise intention.

Then she remembered those eyes, and how pretty she felt every time Patrick looked at her in his hopeful way. She snapped her gaze to the stairs that led down to the gym and quickened her pace.

PATRICK MADE IT back to Chinatown right on time with the exact hardware he'd needed, snagging the best parking space on the block.

Because *everything happens for a reason.* Because whenever a seeming catastrophe struck, awesome stuff resulted.

Like when he'd gotten himself and Steph trapped in the gym—and they'd wound up messing around.

And when his timing belt snapped, who should he end up spending the night with? Maybe he hadn't slept great, but he'd gotten an amazing deal on some mechanical work he'd needed to have done anyhow. And here he was, at his job site at exactly the same time as he would have arrived had the previous day gone to plan. Fate.

Though fate hadn't yet revealed to him why his failed marriage and suffocating mortgage were good things…but the bigger the disaster, the bigger the pay-off, surely, and so the longer the wait.

He already knew intellectually that it was best that he and his ex were through, and his heart was getting closer to believing it, too. Just what opportunity would come along to cement that fact, he couldn't guess yet… Though he did have to wonder if perhaps said opportunity might not have red hair and a supremely skeptical set of matching eyebrows.

He smiled as he carried his tools into the building, feeling warm and pleasantly stupid from his crush. It didn't even matter that she wasn't that into him. It was so joyful just to *feel* this for someone again. To know he hadn't lost it, or used it up, or outgrown it.

He peeked in the Spark windows and found both matchmakers at their desks, no clients in sight. He knocked on the door frame. "Morning."

Jenna smiled. "Good morning, Patrick. The back room's all yours until we lock up at five. Any chance you might be able to finish the job by then?"

"Barring a crisis, yeah." He didn't bother mentioning that crises weren't exactly unheard of where he and electrical work were concerned.

He got set up in the meeting room, snaking a cable out to the main office, which made closing the door impossible. "Sorry in advance if I'm distracting you girls," he said, immediately wondering if these modern women might take offense at being called "girls."

Neither seemed to notice. They got to work when he did, typing on their laptops as he managed to turn off the meeting room's breakers without causing a floor-wide blackout.

How about that? Maybe it was only when Steph was in the vicinity that disasters decided to befall him.

The girls broke for lunch at one, Lindsey kindly asking if she could pick something up for Patrick. Buying lunch hadn't been in his budget lately, but since he'd had no chance to pack one, he gave her a few dollars and she returned shortly with their sandwiches and soup.

Jenna waved him over, rolling out a chair so he could eat with them.

"Good day for chowder," she said as he lifted the lid of his container.

"Tell me about it. Have you heard the forecast? Feels like snow."

She nodded. "Three to six inches, they said."

Maybe it would turn into a storm by the early evening, and he'd wind up taking refuge at Steph's again, once her second date with the hot doctor got snowed out… Hey, a man could hope.

"How's the back room coming?" Jenna asked.

"Right on track. Way easier job than the basement. You should see the wiring down there."

"Excellent. We need to get that space in shape—we're way overdue to hire another matchmaker, but we've got no place to put one at the moment."

"So, Patrick," Lindsey piped up from her desk.

"Yeah?"

"Since we've got you in our lair, I can only imagine it's appropriate to ask if you're single."

He smiled tightly. "I'm divorced, yeah."

"In the market for a nice young lady?" Lindsey asked, bobbing her eyebrows. Her boss shot her a stern look that she ignored.

"I am, yeah. But I can't afford you guys, I'm afraid. Plus I'm not exactly Spark material. Steph said you guys found her some fancy doctor."

"Any well-adjusted, professional guy without a serious criminal record is Spark material," Lindsey said.

"Well, if I happen to win a membership in a raffle or something, I'll be sure to sign up. I could use all the help I can get."

"Oh?"

He nodded, stirring his soup. "Dating feels completely different after being off the market for half a decade. The technology aspect alone."

Jenna lit up like he'd said the magic word. "I am so with you there."

"Steph said you guys don't encourage texting with the people you get set up with."

She shook her head, chewing, and Lindsey said slyly, "You and Steph talk a lot."

He was spared having to reply when Jenna spoke. "We like our clients to approach their love lives as seriously as they would an important job interview. And you wouldn't text your prospective boss to set up a meeting."

"No, definitely not." And a woman who signed up for this service would surely be serious about finding a partner, then.

He set his spoon down. "Can I ask you a dating-conundrum-type question?"

"Always," Jenna said.

"So I'm like, broke."

"Okay."

"Do I even have any business trying to date right now? Or should I wait until I have more to offer? Does a guy have to come standard with a good job to be dateable?"

"Not if the woman's rich," Lindsey offered, and was shot another look by her boss.

"I'd say *a job,* period, should be standard," Jenna said. "Or at least the education or training that would help a person find one. Stability is important. Not just to a potential mate, either. It should be important to you, trying to get yourself to a better place with your finances."

"Of course."

"I can tell you from experience, I grew up pretty poor, until my mom met my stepdad. He wasn't rich or anything, and he had to know what he was signing up for, getting involved with a struggling single mom and her kid. But he didn't make that choice based on what was the smartest move for himself."

"And it worked out?"

Jenna nodded. "We ended up pretty comfortable by the time I went to college. And if not for his support while my mom went back to school, she never would have gotten that chance."

"Gotcha." So in this equation, Patrick was Jenna's mom...just with a beast of a mortgage instead of a kid. It seemed a bit of a tough sell, this scenario, with the genders reversed. "So there's hope, is what you're saying."

"Sure. Love makes people illogical in the best way," she concluded with a smile. "And sometimes our least logical decisions wind up being in our best interest."

Love. That was a hell of a lot to wish for in the Steph department. But hope—hope was good.

Patrick felt hopeful about the future in general. What choice did a guy have, aside from *hoping* things would get better? *Assuming* they would, and doing the work to move in that direction? He didn't understand people who just rolled over and gave up. He'd take any job—bartending, sanitation, cold-calling strangers to sell them stuff they didn't need—before he'd ever *give up.* Maybe he'd get fore-closed on someday, but at least if he did, he wouldn't suffer any regrets, worrying maybe he hadn't done everything he could to fight it.

"I'm hopeful," he concluded.

"Good. That's all you need," Jenna said. "Hope and determination."

"Plus no one is *ever* in perfect shape in every aspect of their life," Lindsey added. "No one goes into a search for a mate a hundred percent ready. As long as you're not like, crippled by the weight of your issues, or motivated by the wrong intentions, you're as ready as anyone could hope to be."

"Huh." That was probably true enough.

Not wanting to take too generous a lunch break, Patrick polished off his chowder and sandwich and thanked the women for their company, then got back to work.

Hope and determination, his head echoed. And the best of intentions.

That was his outlook to a T. He trusted it would sort out his debt in time. Why not believe maybe it could work for his love life, too? What were his intentions? What did he hope to gain, and how could he point himself in that direction?

A minor shock jolted down his arm as he tweaked the wiring, and he swore under his breath, shaking out his hand. But in its wake, he had his answer. Hope plus determination, and a plan… Yeah. He could do that.

8

THE FOLLOWING FRIDAY dawned icy cold. Where was global warming when you needed it?

Steph was running late for the noontime jujitsu session she was due to lead, and a jog to work might be her only chance at feeling even remotely warmed up. She crunched her way across the bridge and aimed herself toward Chinatown, gym bag flopping at her butt.

Her second date with Dr. Dylan the previous week had proved a complete fizzle. Again, he was perfectly charming, but the buzz of anticipation she'd felt during their first dinner was gone. She knew how Patrick made her feel now, and no amount of hoping could replicate it with Dylan. It simply wasn't there.

She'd cut him off before the good-night kiss with "This has been really lovely...but I'm just not feeling it. I'm sorry." And he'd stiffened, thanked her for the second date, and said good-night. He hadn't walked her to her door this time, but she couldn't blame him.

She'd had two more first dates earlier this week, orchestrated by Jenna; one with a PhD candidate and one with a man who did something-or-other in finance. Nice enough guys, but again, no physical connection. A couple of chaste good-night kisses had told her all she'd needed to know. Patrick had set the bar perilously high on the chemistry front, and she wasn't willing to waste the time of any man who couldn't clear it, no matter *how* great he looked on paper.

Her chances at scoring a polished and pedigreed emergency wedding date were looking bleak. It'd take a miracle at this point. But who knew—perhaps that miracle would be one of the twenty bachelors Jenna had selected for the Spark mixer happening the following evening.

The preceding weekend had been fun at least, eaten up by a two-day beginners' seminar for new and prospective Wilinski's members. Steph had been pleased to see three young women in attendance. By the end of the Sunday session, all of them seemed eager to join, once the women's facilities were finalized. Wilinski's would be joining the twenty-first century in no time. She smiled at the thought, breath puffing white clouds into the icy morning air.

Worries over her tardiness dissolved as she mounted the building's front steps. Jenna had a client waiting—a male client. He was sitting on the foyer's loveseat before a fancy floral arrangement, flipping through a magazine. Steph's curiosity was piqued. Too bad she looked like such a harried mess. But as she hauled the heavy glass door open—

Patrick Doherty. Again. But dressed in a chocolate-brown sweater and cleaner jeans than she was used to seeing him in. His shoes had been shined.

Oh *no*. He'd joined Spark.

She wasn't sure which possibility pickled her stomach worse—that he'd joined, thinking it'd gain him access to her, or that she might have to imagine him kissing other women. Stylish women. Spark-worthy women, her competition at tomorrow night's mixer.

Patrick spotted her as the door eased shut and hopped to his feet, tossing the magazine aside. "Steph, hey!"

"Hi, Patrick." She clutched her bag's strap, wary. He

wasn't equipped to endanger her safety, for once, but his presence after an entire week's radio silence was…confusing.

More confusing still, he picked up the vase of flowers and held it out. Their Technicolor shades turned his irises blue as a postcard ocean.

She eyed the arrangement, pulling off her mittens. "Are those for me?"

"You um, you said it was your birthday this week. When I gave you a lift."

"It's my birthday today." She'd forgotten until just now, so preoccupied with the time

"Hey, perfect! Happy birthday."

So if he wasn't here for a Spark appointment, then why? Though his clothes already answered the question, she asked it anyway. "Are you doing another job for Jenna?" She looked to the office windows, finding the blinds mercifully shut, no matchmaker eyes recording this exchange.

"Nope. I just came to give you these."

"Why?"

His smile wilted some and he lowered the vase. "Because I like you."

Her eyes told him volumes. *Did you not hear any of the things I made perfectly clear last Thursday evening?* She'd thought he had. Yet here he was.

"I haven't had a crush on anybody in ages," he said quietly. "I know I'm probably never getting anyplace serious with you, but can't I bring you flowers for your birthday? I swear I'm not a stalker. I just had the day off, and figured…" He trailed off, deflated.

She pursed her lips.

"They can be friendly flowers, if you want. It just feels good, liking somebody again. That's all. I've been looking forward to giving you these all week."

She shoved her mittens in her pockets and accepted the

flowers. They were gorgeous—bright tropical colors, the arrangement bursting with calla and tiger lilies. This was no ten-dollar drugstore bouquet, and Patrick wasn't in a position to be splashing out on flowers. "You shouldn't have. But you did, and they're beautiful. Thank you."

"It was my pleasure. My neighbor snuck some money into my mailbox for snowblowing her driveway, so I figured, hey—unexpected windfall, may as well use it for an unexpected gift for Steph."

She pictured him dashing from his truck to the building, dodging ice, coat hugged around the arrangement to shield it from the frigid wind. "I'll have to keep them at work. They'll never survive the walk home."

"I could drive you later."

She gave him a stern look, making it clear there was a line that separated *endearing* from *pushy*. And clarity was in short supply where her feelings for Patrick were concerned.

"Or not."

"Thank you, really. I don't doubt your intentions." Oh Lord, she had a suitor with honorable intentions. What century was she living in? "But please…let me decide whether or not to call you, okay?"

He smiled tightly. "Sure."

"I have to lead a session now."

"That's cool. Have a great birthday, Steph."

"Thanks." She cradled the vase to her side with one arm, and gave his shoulder an apologetic squeeze. "Take care."

She left him in the foyer, heading down the steps to the gym without a backward glance.

She must seem so cold. But if she let him know how torn she felt, how badly she wanted him deep down… Hope seemed a cruel gift to give Patrick, when she couldn't say for sure if it was her heart or her libido that found him magnetic. He offered his emotions so freely. It'd be unfair to lead him on when she had no clue what she was after anymore.

"Oh ho," Rich said as she entered the gym, spotting her flowers.

She pushed her sneakers off at the door. "Who you calling a ho, Estrada?"

He abandoned the spray bottle he'd been using on the mats to follow her to the lounge. "Well done, mystery doctor."

"They're not from the doctor. Me and the doctor didn't pan out. None of my Spark dates have panned out yet."

"Bummer. Who're they from, then?"

"They're just birthday flowers." She made Rich hold them as she unfolded a card table beside the recliners. The recliners where she and Patrick had first kissed. Facing the TV he'd installed, in this room where he'd nearly broken her nose the second they met.

Rich set the vase on the table. "Pretty fancy birthday flowers."

Steph dropped her bag by the wall and ditched her hat and coat. "They're from an admirer, if you must know."

"Oh? Not a gym member, I hope."

She hopped on one foot, stripping her sock. "Just this guy I keep running into."

"You think it'll turn into anything serious?"

She sighed and eyed the clock on the DVD player, finding she still had a few minutes before the session officially started. "I don't even know what we are."

His brow rose. "I see."

"No, you don't. Even *I* don't see what's going on, so you sure as heck don't."

"Do you like this guy?" Rich asked.

"I do… But he's not exactly relationship material."

"In what way?"

She dropped onto a recliner and tugged off the other

sock. "I grew up kinda broke, and I don't exactly make a ton as a trainer."

"Tell me about it."

"If I keep doing what I love, what I'm supposed to be doing, I'm *never* going to be especially comfortable, financially."

He nodded, looking uncharacteristically serious.

"And this guy's struggling to even pay his mortgage. I *do* like him. He's a really good guy. And our chemistry is like, ridiculous. At first I thought he was too much like all the dudes I dated in my twenties, but now…I don't really care about that. Dating a doctor was a flop, in the end. But what I *do* care about is not signing up to struggle for the rest of my life. Is that awful?"

Rich shook his head. "I used to feel the same way. I was determined not to settle down until I knew all my family shit was squared away, finances-wise."

"Surely it is now." Rich had to be in the upper quarter of professional fighters as far as paydays and promo ops went.

"More or less. But when Lindsey and I started up, I wasn't there yet. And I was determined not to fall for her, not until I had everything nailed down. But we kept colliding…"

He eyed Steph's recliner in a way that made her wonder if she wasn't the first trainer to compromise the honor of this room. Probably best not to think too hard about that.

"And you just knew, at a certain point, that your logical plans could shove it?"

He sank into the other chair. "Kind of. Or I realized that even though she complicated my plans, she also offered me way more stuff in return—enough to cancel out the fact that I'd have to rearrange everything to make room for her. Hell, to abandon a bunch of really amazing opportunities out west, to come back here for good."

"How'd you know?"

"I was just unhappy away from her. She has this weird way of like, venting all the ugly, dark shit that weighs me down sometimes. I didn't even make it a week, when I moved out to California. It was like moving into a cave, all cold and gloomy."

"Awww." Steph reached out to give his shoulder a teasing punch. "You've gone soft."

"I'm okay with that."

"Did you think you were in love with her by the time you made that decision?"

"I wasn't sure. I hadn't been in love before. But I knew it was something special."

Something special. Her and Patrick's physical connection certainly felt special. He seemed tailor-made for her sexually.

"I don't know what to do."

"Obviously, if you're asking *me* for advice."

"He really likes me. And I *do* like him. I'm just scared of what a future with him would look like. And I don't want to lead him on, keeping one foot in the door." She groaned, rubbing her face.

"Would you rather be poor and happy, or rich and dissatisfied?"

"I want to be rich and happy."

He grinned. "Touché."

"And struggling can suck the happiness right out of even the strongest relationship."

Rich nodded. "I'm not drunk, so I won't get all sloppy and tell you exactly why I'm totally with you on the not-wanting-to-be-poor front. I'll just say that there's something to be said for financial stability, but there's also something to be said for the emotional stability that the right person can offer. But at the end of the day, only your gut can tell you which is more important."

"It's hard to hear my gut with my brain and my libido arguing so loudly."

"Give it a while. Date some more of those fancy dudes Jenna trades in. And if they all leave you cold, and it's meant to be with the mystery pauper... He'll still be around in a few weeks."

She nodded. It was solid advice. And a game plan dished out by a trainer—she could trust that process, at least. "Thanks. This was helpful."

Rich stood. "Consider it your birthday present. Hey, you up for after-sparring drinks, or you got a hot date already? Maybe I could get drunk and sloppy after all."

"No, no dates. No drinks, either, though. I'm getting burned out on the bar scene. Need to conserve my stamina for this Spark mixer tomorrow night."

"I'll see you tomorrow morning, right? Around eleven?"

She nodded. He'd invited her to brunch, to get to know Lindsey better and check out her apartment. "The way you talk about your mom's cooking, I wouldn't miss it. I better get class started." She got up to pull her *gi* from her bag, ushering Rich out the door so she could change.

She tried to get lost in the day's sessions, lost in the mechanics of her body. But her body was a traitor today, taunting her with memories of that night last week with Patrick. It refused to let her take Rich's advice and put Patrick on the back burner. Their attraction couldn't be expected to simply simmer—it was boil or nothing.

The thought of the mixer—and the dates that might follow with guys who weren't Patrick Doherty—brought no excitement, no anticipation. Only exhaustion. It made her think maybe there *was* hope for the current generation, with its fear of commitment, fear of missing out. It seemed Steph's body had decided she'd found The One, and the thought of auditioning any other man left her cold.

Maybe this is what you need right now.

Maybe she needed exactly what Patrick offered—a relationship rooted solely in the now, no pressure over what might come. After all, everything else in her life was about to settle—a steady job, a fixed residence. Maybe wanting to find something long-term on top of all that would prove too much commitment, too fast. She was only thirty, after all. Exactly thirty. There was still time to meet someone, whether her biological clock wanted her to believe that or not. There was still a *little* time left for sexual freedom, as she eased into her new life.

Mercer arrived, as did the late-afternoon lull. Steph eyed him, thinking she'd already heard Rich's take on the situation, and of the two of them, Mercer had more in common with Patrick. They were cast from the same hardworking, level-headed mold. She crossed to where he was mending the padding along the top of the octagon's fence.

He smiled as she wandered into the ring. "Heading home, birthday girl?"

"Pretty soon. Think I'm too wiped for sparring tonight."

"Any big plans?"

"None, but I'm fine with that. Can I um… Could I ask your opinion, as a dude?"

He shrugged. "Shoot."

She leaned into the chain link, avoiding his eyes. "Say you'd been having this casual sort of fling with a woman…"

"Okay."

"And you really like her, but you're not really supposed to be hooking up, but you keep winding up together, anyway…"

He laughed. "It's amazing how easy I can imagine this hypothetical scenario."

Steph wondered if he meant Jenna. If so, did that mean Steph's so-called romance expert had let her sex drive make the occasional ill-informed decision?

"Well, say you really liked this woman, and she knew it.

But she keeps telling you she's not ready for anything serious with you. She's been nothing but forthright about it, but you tell her you'd be happy just to keep messing around, like you have been…"

"You wanna know if the woman would be a selfish jerk if she took the guy up on his offer?"

"Yeah."

Mercer smiled, ripping a length of black duct tape from its roll. "What makes you think the guy isn't secretly relieved that the woman's not after something serious?"

She pictured those gorgeous flowers in the lounge, and that naked excitement and hope in Patrick's eyes every time he spotted her. "He just isn't the type."

"Well," Mercer said, "I think most guys would happily take sex as a consolation prize, even if they wanted something more. Maybe for a woman, it would be insulting, make them feel like they got used. But for a guy, I bet sex would soften the blow."

"So this woman wouldn't be guilty of taking advantage of the guy's crush or whatever?"

"Not if the guy knew the deal."

"Right. Good."

Mercer smirked, smoothing another strip of tape in place. "It's your birthday, Steph. Go get laid. I promise you this guy's not going to sob into his pillow after you leave, *disappointed* he got used for sex."

She grinned. "Thanks, boss."

"I'm not your boss. Jenna is. And trust me—she's got no right to lecture a woman about taking advantage of a defenseless man. So go nuts."

Steph headed back to the lounge. She packed her workout clothes away and stared at her phone, rubbing the screen with her thumb. With a deep breath, she dug out her wallet, finding Patrick's card. She dialed his number with her heart in her throat.

"Patrick Doherty."

"Hey, it's Steph."

"Oh. Hey." There was worry in his voice. This call could easily be in the vein of, *Listen, pal—leave me alone or I'll sic my huge colleagues on your stalker ass.*

"Hey. Um… Would you like to hang out sometime?"

Silence for a breath, then, "Sure. What kind of hanging out?"

"Like a date, I guess. A casual one. Like last week."

"Really?"

"Yeah. You've heard my concerns a dozen times, but I *do* like you. And I like what happens when we hang out, just for what it is. And I'd kind of like for it to happen again, maybe after dinner or something."

"Wow… *Wow.* Awesome. I'd love that. Where do you want to go? It'll have to be someplace kinda cheap—"

"I'm sick of going out. Would you like to come over for dinner and a movie some night?"

"How about tonight?"

"I just finished work, and I'm all gross. And I don't own a TV, so the movie's kind of out."

"I'll pick you up. You can come to my place."

"Maybe…" She was free the next morning, until that brunch at Rich's. She could afford a late night.

"Come on, you had to work on your thirtieth birthday! You shouldn't have to make your own dinner, too."

She eyed the clock. It was still early. "Give me 'til six-thirty so I can go home and get cleaned up, then okay. You're on."

"Awesome!"

"Just call when you pull up. See you in a bit."

"You will indeed," he said, his smile audible.

She turned her phone off, surprised not to find any of the *what-have-I-just-done?* dread dogging her. In fact, she felt relieved, having committed to this baby step. And less guilty, knowing she was doing the fair thing, giving Patrick the same chance she'd offered the guys from Spark. The battle between logic and lust was likely far from resolved, but at least her gut felt settled, for the moment.

Maybe Patrick would lose some of his allure now that their date was for real. His forbidden-fruit appeal would be gone, and maybe without that clouding her decisions and seducing her reason away, she'd find they actually weren't compatible. Maybe it'd all prove a non-issue.

Or maybe they'd fall wildly in love and just live in starry-eyed poverty for the rest of their lives, too happy to care that they couldn't afford to start a family.

A departing gym member who lived in South Boston was nice enough to drop Steph at her place so she was able to get her flowers home. The lilies were pungent, filling her tiny apartment with the smell of the South Pacific.

By the time her hair was dry and her pitiful arsenal of makeup tricks exhausted, snow was flurrying outside her window.

She wanted what Patrick could offer—easy, casual company—so she didn't bother dressing for a date. A pair of stretchy black pants, a tee and a long duster sweater. Clothes for lounging on a couch, watching a movie, maybe eating dinner off plates set on their laps, chatting. Later, kissing. Later still… Well, she'd trust her gut on that one, too. Trying to logic her way through the situation these last couple weeks had led to nothing but confusion and doubt. No more thinking. She hugged herself, watching the flakes swirl like gold dust in the yellow streetlights.

Her buzzer sounded and she hurried over to press the button. "Be down in a minute."

Funny, she thought as she zipped her jacket and flipped off the lights. She'd been picked up by both of her Spark dates this week, and both had texted to announce their arrival. Supposedly well-pedigreed guys…

And yet it was the under-employed carpenter who took the time to brave the cold and ring her bell.

As she walked to the elevator, she felt it in every step— excitement. This time last week she'd made this same trip, heading down to meet Dylan for their second date, and all she'd felt then was misgiving. The seemingly right sort of man, who made her feel all wrong.

She punched the button for the lobby.

And when the door slid open again, there he was.

The exactly wrong sort of man, with that smile that made her feel so damn right.

9

STEPH RETURNED PATRICK'S smile, excitement and nerves clashing in her belly. "Hey."

"Hey." As he leaned in to give her a chivalrous cheek-kiss, she could smell winter on his skin and in his hair.

"You could've just called, you know. And stayed in your nice warm truck."

"And waste all these chances to woo you?" He held the foyer door for her.

The truck was idling a few spaces down. He opened her side and Steph tossed her overnight bag behind their seats.

"Thanks for coming all this way to pick me up," she said as they slammed their doors.

"My pleasure."

"Was it a long drive?"

He turned them onto the road. "Little over an hour, with the traffic."

"Oh jeez. You must have left right after we hung up." She eyed his ensemble—no coat or gloves or hat to be seen. He must've practically launched himself out the door, teeth chattering for the first couple miles, as he waited for the truck to warm up.

He grinned in the red glow of a traffic light. "I was eager."

"What'd you do all day?"

"Well, I spent forever trying to pick out the perfect flowers for this woman I have a crush on."

She had to smile. And since she'd given him permission to revel in said crush for the duration of this date, it was nice to not feel compelled to quash his eagerness. "They're lovely. My apartment smells like Bora Bora."

"Then I delivered them and totally struck out, so I went home and job-searched for a few hours. And it all came to naught and I was really depressed, except then the woman I like called to ask me out. So actually it turned out to be the best day ever."

She shook her head, smiling. "You are treacherously adorable." *And your wife was a fool.* If Steph were making as much money as he'd implied his ex had been, she'd be only too happy to support a partner as lovable as this man.

You don't know her, though. And you barely know Patrick. It was easy to make these judgments with only the most basic facts and stupefying lust to guide her.

They made easy small talk on the drive, about the North Shore and the pros and cons of living in a summer town.

As they pulled into Patrick's driveway, Steph could hear the ocean. His house was a long one-story plus a pitched live-in attic, a Cape Cod with the requisite thick wooden shingles.

"Have you considered renting your place out during the tourist season?" she asked as they unbuckled their seat belts. "And crashing with family for the summer? You could probably make more than you pay for your mortgage."

"Double it, I imagine," he said, and opened his door, getting her bag from behind the seats. "I didn't have my shit together last summer—the divorce chaos interrupted my plans to refinish the floors halfway through the job. But if I haven't been foreclosed on by the time May rolls around, it's a great option."

"You wouldn't mind strangers staying in your home, with all the work you've put into it?" she asked as they clomped up the steps to his ocean-view deck.

"Not at all. I'm proud of my home. And waterfront's at such a premium around here, I like the idea of some poor landlocked family getting to borrow all this for a few weeks."

He opened the sliding doors at the back of the house and waved Steph into a cozy sunroom. She pushed her boots off in the corner, inspecting the space when Patrick switched on the lights. Nothing flashy at first glance, but the walls were lined with recessed shelving, full of books and board games and photo frames and keepsakes.

"Wow," she said, taking it all in. "Did you do the shelves?"

"I did. And all the crown molding." He pointed to the elegant woodwork adorning the seams where the ceiling met the walls. "This place was a real fixer-upper. The ocean's not exactly a carpenter's best friend, but it's worth the work for that view."

"I'm sure. Especially if you enjoy the work."

His smile confirmed what she already knew—he loved the work. And that love for one's craft was what kept Steph waking up, eager to train, despite all the aches and bruises and stitches *her* passion offered as rewards for her dedication.

He led the way into the next room, a large den. Steph rubbed her arms. "It's freezing in here."

Patrick set her bag on a couch and went to the wall, flipping up the thermostat panel. "I know, sorry. Money's so tight, I've been turning the heat way down and bundling up. I didn't think to crank it before I left to grab you."

"Your pipes could freeze."

"I keep the taps dripping." He shut the panel and rolled up his sleeves, turning his attention to the brick fireplace opposite a big picture window.

"You're making a fire? Cool."

"It's your birthday—of course I'll build you a fire."

She watched as he did. Strong shoulders, solid frame, forearms twitching as he arranged the kindling and logs.

How had she even gotten here? He hadn't coerced her, yet she'd resisted him the entire way. He'd seduced her somehow. With his kindness and charm, his handsome face and the memories burned onto her libido from the way her body matched his.

"What's for dinner?" she asked.

"I'm only good at about five things, and I've only got the ingredients for one of them. You down with macaroni and cheese?"

She laughed. "Powdered or Velveeta?"

He smiled over his shoulder, dimples flashing. "I'm not *that* ghetto."

Once the fire was crackling, he led her to a homey dine-in kitchen. Its light bathed the tall, brittle grass and the sand outside in a warm glow.

"Get comfy. You want a drink? I've got beers, and my sister left a couple bottles of wine last time she visited."

Steph took a seat at the table. "I'll try your sister's wine."

He rummaged and brought out two reds from a pantry. "I'm sure they're good. She's got good taste in stuff like that."

Steph picked a bottle at random and Patrick uncorked it, filling a blue plastic picnic goblet for her.

"I know the stemware's hideous," he said, handing it over. "I lost the real stuff in the divorce."

"I promise I couldn't care less." She sipped the wine. A bit dry, but every time she had expensive wine at restaurants, it was dry like this. She bet a person with a half-decent palate would say it was great. "It's great," she decided aloud.

Patrick cracked open a beer and got to work. He boiled fat pasta shells, stirred them with butter in a baking dish. The cheesy component he made out of cheddar, cream, more butter, a few spices and an egg, stirring it all in and topping it with breadcrumbs and pepper. It was a heart-attack casserole, but a side effect of Steph's job was that she could eat pretty much whatever she wanted.

"Should be about thirty minutes," Patrick said, shutting the oven door and setting the timer.

"It already smells amazing."

He grabbed her wine from the counter and led her back to his den. "My TV's hooked up to the web, so you've got your choice of anything we can stream."

They got settled on the couch and Steph was entrusted with the remote. She found them a high-budget Hollywood action movie neither had seen, and hit Play.

Patrick smiled at her. "This feels familiar. Only we're not locked in a gym and I don't have to read any subtitles."

She blushed, knowing neither the fire nor the wine had any part in the heat warming her face. It was Patrick, and how pleasant it felt, being close to him. How easy. And yet how exciting.

"Thank you for having me over," she said after a time, speaking to her glass.

"Thanks for coming."

She met his eyes. "I know I've been nothing but cagey toward you."

"Well, I've been nothing but pushy."

She shook her head, smiling. "No. I hate being pushed around." *Outside of the bedroom, anyhow.* "So I know it's not that. Just eager. And open. I still have no clue how I feel about dating at the moment, but you deserve a fair shake."

"Because I wore you down?"

She laughed. "Maybe."

He took her hand, twining their fingers, and that easy warmth spread through her body.

He squeezed her fingers. "I'll take it."

Before their mouths met, their noses brushed. Then the lightest touch of his lips, the soft scrape of his stubble. He let her hand go to palm her jaw, and the world dissolved.

Oh, these kisses, the ones that haunted her at night. Every time their mouths came together, she was blown away anew by the intensity of this connection. And tonight there was something different. A tenderness layered beneath the passion, his touch making her feel cradled and coveted at once. A touch that welcomed trust even as it promised ferocity. A sensuality that—

BRRRRRUUUUZZZZZZZZ.

She gasped at the metallic wail of the oven timer, hand flying to her chest.

Patrick laughed and got to his feet. "You okay?"

"*Jesus.* Are we ever going to enjoy a make-out session that's not interrupted by a phone or a door buzzer or an alarm?"

Smiling, he jogged to the kitchen. Over the ringing he shouted, "Come serve yourself."

They ate just as she'd imagined, off their laps, watching the movie. Or half watching the movie. She couldn't be sure about Patrick, but Steph's attention was still glued firmly to her couchmate.

"That was delicious," she said as he took her empty bowl, stacking it atop his on the coffee table. "Thank goodness I don't have to track my carbs anymore."

He grabbed her legs behind the knees, just as he had in the gym, and pulled her calves across his lap. He squeezed her feet in turn, and met her eyes with his blue ones. "I'm really glad you came over."

"Me, too. It's turned into a really nice birthday."

He plucked at her pants, making the soft, stretchy fabric snap back against her shin. "I couldn't help but notice you dressed for a sleepover."

Her expression turned shifty. "Maybe."

"Are you staying the night?"

She ignored the warm flush creeping up her neck. "I couldn't very well ask you to drive me back to Boston this late."

He smiled. "Of course you could."

The blush burned even hotter. *I could. And you'd do it, wouldn't you?* He'd do anything she asked, just for the pleasure of feeling useful. Or needed. *You really are the kindest man I've ever met.* "I'm not going to ask you to."

"No?"

"No. I'd like to stay the night."

He grinned, the skin beside his eyes crinkling with mischief. "Oh good."

Again, that old misgiving… She needed reassurance that they were on the same page. "I feel like a jerk even saying this, but…this is still just casual, okay? Anything that happens tonight." Of course Patrick was okay with it—she'd laid it out for him enough times. So who was she really worried was in danger of losing sight of the facts?

He smiled. "I'm okay for a tumble, but not anything serious?" There was a tease in his tone, telling her he still knew the score, much as it disappointed him. He took her hand. "It's fine. You're allowed to have standards."

"It's not that I only want to date guys who'll take me fancy places, or have nice cars or apartments. It's not because a guy isn't *good* enough…" She struggled to find a way to explain that sounded even half-valid. Patrick found one for her.

"Security's important, I know. If you didn't want to date a guy who was a stunt driver, or an alligator wrestler, or a gambling addict or whatever, nobody would judge you. They shouldn't judge you for not wanting to get serious with a guy who's a financial risk, either."

"I never realized, growing up, that some people didn't have to worry about bills. That they made more than they needed. And now that I have, I just *want* that so much." A life free of money stress. She pictured her parents, their backs as they sat together at the dining room table late at night, obsessing in hushed voices over which utilities to pay that month.

Patrick let her hand go with a final squeeze. "I get that, I promise. I knew all this going in, and I kept at you anyway. I want whatever you're offering."

"And *I* know...what you told me, about why your wife decided to leave."

He smiled tightly. "I won't lie—it's a sore spot. But I know the score with you. We're not exactly walking down the aisle and promising we'll be there for rich or for poor. If you've been anything with me from the start, it's blunt. About not being interested in me."

"And yet here I am."

He wiggled his eyebrows, grinning. Damn those dimples.

"I still feel a bit tacky. Telling you I'm happy to mess around with you, even if I won't date you."

"I think you might find that guys don't get too bent out of shape about that kind of stuff when you're offering them sex."

"So I've been told." She put her hands to his jaw, stoking his sideburns with her thumbs. "I do love you simple creatures."

"I'm as simple as they come, so that's fine by me."

"Do you want to maybe show me your room...?"

Another of those brain-dismantling grins, and he let her

legs go. Once the TV was shut off, he took her hand, drawing her off the couch and down a short hall.

"Bathroom," he said as they passed it, en route to the door at the end. "And the bedroom."

He flipped on the lights as they entered.

She took in his bed, much bigger than her own, and made, if somewhat hastily. This room felt so cozy, with snow falling beyond the old windows, so pretty against the black sea and sky. She paused to study everything—the molding around the closet door, the wainscoting, the shelving along one wall. The bedposts and headboard, also clearly handcrafted, everything stained the same rich brown, dark as espresso.

"Did you do *all* this? All the woodworking in here? And the finishing?"

He smiled, nodding.

She crossed the room to run her hand along the windowsill—even those had been redone, the wood meeting the wall with an elegant scalloped bevel. "Wow." She whipped her head around to stare at him. "You really are a great carpenter."

He laughed. "I'm a shitty electrician, but I'm not a liar."

That seemed true enough. Honest, sweet, humble. Patrick Doherty to a tee.

"Your numb fingertips are suddenly starting to seem worth it. This is amazing."

"You ever need some work done, I'm at your service."

"If I ever wake up a homeowner, you'll be the first one I call. Not that I think I'd be able to afford you, seeing all this."

"I'll give you a good rate."

"I'm sure you would…" But there was something else she needed from him tonight. A different sort of craft, performed by those talented hands. She felt the smile curling her lips, pure mischief.

"What?" he asked, eyes twinkling.

"Take me to bed, Patrick." *Take me. Own me. Boss me.* She held too much power over this man. She'd be happy to surrender some, shed it alongside their clothing.

He took her hand and led her to the bedside. Without a word, he unbuttoned her sweater, lifted her shirt, eased her pants down her legs. He unclasped her bra and silently slipped it from her shoulders. Those blue eyes lingered and studied and memorized, making her feel like the most fascinating woman in the world, then his hands joined the exploration. He stroked her shoulders and arms, dropping to his knees as he reached her hips. Soft kisses tickled her navel, and she drew her nails across his scalp as his palms kneaded her butt and thighs.

When he stood, she returned the treatment, undressing him slowly, all the way down to his boxers. They climbed onto the bed together, kissing and fondling, taking their time in a way they hadn't that night on her couch.

He coaxed her hand downward, cupping her palm to his hard length through the velvety, worn cotton of his boxers. Her breath drew short as she curved her fingers around him, curious and eager. His hips shifted and he moved his hand to her waist, savoring her touch with a soft moan.

"That feels good."

Was it wrong to assume she was the first woman to be with him this way, since his divorce…and selfish to be taking such pleasure from it? Maybe. Did she care? Not a bit. It felt like a gift she could give him. To be the first to make him feel like a man again this way. To offer him a grateful woman's body, even if she couldn't offer her heart.

"*You* feel good," she corrected, giving him a long, measuring stroke.

He moaned. Then his warm, strong hand clasped hers, forcing tight, slow pulls. Her pulse hammered, spurred by his bossiness.

"I can't tell you how many times I've thought about you."

"You, too." *Though I didn't mean to. And perhaps I shouldn't be telling you now.* Too late.

"What's it like, when you imagine it?" he asked.

"Like that night at my place. Only…more."

"You were amazing. The way you… Just your mouth. And how physical you are. You made me feel so spoiled."

The words set her on fire. She wanted that, exactly that—to make this man feel spoiled. And needed. And *obeyed.*

She tugged at his shorts, and he pushed them down. As she stroked his cock, he slipped his hand inside her panties, exploring with the softest caresses.

"Wow," he whispered, fingertips finding her wet. He slicked them along her lips, making her ache for so much more.

"You have condoms?" she asked.

"Yeah." He leaned over, rummaging for a box in his bedside table drawer. To Steph's selfish delight, she heard the tearing of cardboard. This box hadn't yet been opened. She really would be his first since…

She lost the thought, distracted as he turned back, condom in hand. He sheathed himself with a slow stroke. So slow she could make out the trembling of his fingers.

"I like it kind of rough," she murmured, excited to even be articulating the thought. "If you're okay with it."

"I can be anything. How rough, though? Not like, smacking you around or anything, right? I don't think I'd be cool with that."

"No. Just…physical. Bossy. Not mean or angry, just pushy. I like feeling overpowered in bed."

"Sure." He looked delighted to simply be having this talk, cementing the promise of sex. No judgment, no worrying about what her request *meant,* just excitement to have been given an assignment. He really was a lovely man. A book so open, its cover fallen off, all the pages laid out for the world to see.

"Should I say anything special?"

"Say whatever you want. Dirty talk's always welcome. But you don't need to call me names or anything like that. Just don't be gentle."

"Starting now?"

"Whenever you're ready."

"Roger that." He rolled her onto her back, jamming his hips to hers and forcing her thighs wide, cock jabbing her inner thigh.

Dear God, yes.

And with a swift precision she'd never have expected of this man, Patrick fisted the cotton of her panties and ripped them straight down the middle.

Holy shit.

Do that again. Ten thousand times.

His big fingers spread the shredded fabric and she watched with held breath as he angled himself to her folds.

There was friction, but only for the first push or two. As each thick inch of his cock disappeared, the motions became smoother, slicker, easier. The most natural thing in the world.

She stroked his hair and shut her eyes, just feeling him, listening to his strained and heavy breaths.

Finding his stride, he held her hip, easing in and out with growing confidence. His lips brushed hers and she opened her eyes to find those blue ones so close. She accepted his kiss, sweet to start, but soon growing deep and hungry, mirroring the possession she felt each time he pushed inside. With a hand on his hip, she tugged in time with his rhythm, begging for more.

He freed her lips. "Does this feel good? Faster? Slower?"

"Faster."

He paused, chest swelling with quickened breaths, face

flushed with excitement. *We Irish couldn't hide our arousal if we tried,* she thought, knowing her own pale, freckled skin was broadcasting her lust as plainly as his.

"Just tell me if I go too far."

She nodded, already lost in the commands his body issued. He eased all the way out, cruel and slow, then claimed her again with a deep, mean thrust. Her nails bit his back, shocking his hips and making him buck. *Yes.* Sex like fighting—one act of aggression chasing another.

He found his pace. Long, steady thrusts that drew him all the way out, then drove him deep, burying every inch. Thrusts that demanded, *Watch me.* The cotton of her ruined panties teased the uppermost creases of her thighs, fluttering, taunting proof of what this man was capable of.

"Talk to me," she murmured.

"You feel good." His voice was thick, attention clearly divided. He seemed to gather his wits for a few breaths. "I like how you watch."

She slipped a hand between them, clasping his cock with her thumb and forefinger, making a tight ring where their bodies met. His eyes shut with a groan.

"You're big," she told him.

"Yeah." He gave a few frantic thrusts, spurred by the flattery. "Is that what you like?"

"I love it."

"You want it rougher?"

She nodded.

One at a time, he took her hands and moved them above her head. Bracing his weight on one arm, he pinned her wrists with his free hand and owned her with greedy strokes. The excitement sizzled down her body, a low moan making her approval known.

Her reaction thrilled him in turn. His eyes narrowed, bright with fascination and understanding. He must know now, she didn't just want it fast, or dirty, or with the occasional playful swat at her backside. Domination—that's what she craved. Fingertips digging into her skin, hands pinning her, this feeling of being owned by his cock and helpless against his strength. Powerless. She pushed at his hand just to savor the sensation of being held. It wasn't the cruelty she wanted so much as a brazen show of power. To be told by a man's body, *I can take anything I want.* A cocky, crass display of maleness.

He shifted, grasping a forearm in each hand. His weight pinning her was intimidating, but not painful.

"Patrick." It came out thoughtless as a sigh.

"Yeah."

"You feel good."

"Tell me. Tell me how I feel."

"Controlling."

His hips hammered harder, the pressure on her arms growing sharper, darker.

"And greedy."

He moaned at that one, eyes closing. She watched his face for half a minute as he let himself feel the sensations. She felt his hips stutter, coordination lost to pleasure. His eyes opened and his hands released her.

"Turn over."

She moved to her hands and knees, hugging the pillow, offering her body. He pushed back inside with a grunt, hands clasping the flesh at her hips.

"God. You feel so good… But way too soon."

"Patrick." She craned her neck for a glimpse of that body, chest and abdomen and arms all clenched and tense.

"I wanna come, you feel so good."

"You can do whatever you want."

"I want that…" His hips slowed and she could hear his breath coming loud and fast and desperate behind her. "But I want to feel you come even more. That's what I want. Tell me how."

For Steph, stimulation was easily two-thirds mental. It wouldn't take much physical contact to push her over. "Just keep it rough, and touch me."

He tugged her tight against his hips and planted his knees, finding the balance to reach one arm around her waist. She moaned as those rough fingertips touched her clit, stroking, circling, pinching softly.

She swore.

"Yeah." He found his way with the caresses, thrusts ramping back up. "That feel good?"

"Yes."

"You gonna come on my cock, sweetheart?"

She nodded, frantic. The sheer size and coarseness of his fingers would've been enough, but his touch was perfection. Not masterful. A bit sloppy, the perfect mix of commanding and frantic.

"Yes."

"Yeah. Take me." To punctuate the words, he owned her roughly for a dozen manic thrusts. "That's what you like, right? Take me. Feel me."

She felt him, to be sure. Thick, hard, unrelenting. Punishing. She paid this penance happily, and her physical act of submission had another kind of surrender growing ever closer. She gave herself over to nothing more than the reality of this man's sexual demands, pleasure building, tightening, cresting.

"Oh."

"Good. Do it. Come on my cock."

The world shrank to a tight ball of heat and need, emanating from his fingertips, deepened by his mean strokes. She let its gravity pull her under, swallow her whole and flip her inside-out, groaning through the longest, scariest release.

Patrick eased up, fingers going still, cock moving inside her with only the faintest thrusts. "Good," he murmured, and slid his hand up her belly, along her ribs. She could feel his fingers shaking as they traced her spine, feel the muscles of his hips hitching with his breaths. He seemed to wait until she came down from her orgasm, seconds or minutes or hours. Time had become abstract, a force that meant nothing compared to the will of this man's body.

"Good," he said again, and slowly eased out. "On your back."

She obeyed and he planted his hands beside her ribs, took her with a rough, messy push and a groan so deep she felt it ringing through her bones.

"Jesus, you make me feel huge."

She bit her lip to hide a grin. It was what she wanted to do, the power she craved—to make this man feel strong and desired with this sex. With their two bodies. The only thing that held a candle to fighting.

His domination was gone—he was closer to the brink than he'd let on. He was just a desperate man chasing his own pleasure now. She drank him in with eager eyes.

"Let me see it, when you come."

He met her gaze without a word and she saw helplessness behind those heavy lids. It grew and sharpened, and his racing breaths became moans. She recorded every sound, every motion, knowing without a scrap of doubt that this was the most erotic moment of her life.

"Oh God." All at once he pulled out, stripped the latex and fisted his bare cock. He leaned in close enough to press his forehead to hers, and though she didn't get to see it, she felt it—slick heat bathing her belly, the brush of his knuckles as he coaxed every last drop.

"Patrick…"

"Oh." His hand went still save for a tremor, and he fought to catch his breath. When he found the coordination, he reached for his shorts to wipe his come from her skin, cleaning her in gentle strokes. Steph stripped the tattered scraps of her underwear as he jettisoned the boxers, and he flopped down beside her with a mighty sigh.

After a brief silence he announced, "That was awesome."

She smiled up at the ceiling. She'd been stuck in a dry spell the past few months, but nothing compared to the year-plus Patrick had implied. Knowing she'd ended that for him had her feeling powerful and self-satisfied. "Yeah, it was."

As her sweat cooled, Steph snuggled closer to him. From the clear blue, a thought struck her, charged hot with possession and anger.

Who on earth would ever give this man up?

It came too fast for her to hoist her defenses and bat it aside, too fast to avoid the sting of guilt.

You would. You made that clear from the start. You plan on walking away.

But she still felt that fire in her gut, disgust that a woman could have claimed to love this man enough to marry him, promised him forever, then turned her back when life got tough.

I may not be willing to make that promise to this man, Steph thought.

But at least that means I'll never break it, either.

10

SHE WOKE to the faintest, sweetest sensation—a man's lips trailing soft kisses along her arm. She smiled before her eyes even opened, and found his head with her hands, mussing his hair.

"Keep sleeping," he murmured, sounding barely awake himself.

But she was conscious now, and with that consciousness came a surprising revelation—it was nice, waking up here. With Patrick. No panic, no regret. And memories. Memories of how good it felt, surrendering to this man's secret bossy side. And she had the day off, with nowhere to be until—

She sat up straight. "Oh shit. What time is it?"

He reached across her to the bedside table and checked his phone. "Quarter of ten."

"Crap. I'm supposed to be in Lynn at eleven for brunch. Do you have a train schedule?" At least Newburyport and Lynn were on the same line.

She was already kicking at the sheets, but Patrick looped an arm around her waist and pulled her back against him. "Don't be stupid—I'll drive you."

She turned to meet his eyes. "Yeah?"

"Of course." He kissed her forehead, then tossed the down comforter aside and got out of bed. She sat up, hugging the sheets to her chest, and admired his naked body as he dressed. *Enjoy it while it lasts.*

She grabbed a quick shower and dried her hair, and they climbed into his pre-warmed truck with just enough time to get to Lynn on schedule.

She took in Patrick's town as they wound through the narrow streets, past quaint summer businesses and restaurants.

"Is that where you go to strike out with the local ladies?" she asked him as they passed a bar.

"No, no. Mine's way more of a dive than that. Down by the water. Want to go some night?" He glanced sidelong at her. "It's only a few minutes' walk from my place. We could get drunk and dance next to the pool tables."

She smiled dryly. "I'm thirty now. I was kind of hoping my drunken-bar-dancing days were behind me."

"No one's ever too old for drunken dancing. How else would we survive weddings?"

She stared blankly out the window. Kristy's wedding was drawing close, and it was just about official, barring a miracle at tonight's mixer—Steph would have no one to dance with, drunk or otherwise. Not unless some ancient flame from high school asked her. And she knew exactly which pitying look her bitch of a cousin would shoot her, should that wind up the case.

Take what you can get, Penny. You might clean up okay for a tomboy, but I won't be holding my breath, waiting for an invite to your big day.

"Did I say something wrong?" Patrick asked.

"Oh, no. Not at all. Just thinking about a family thing I have to go to next weekend. For this cousin I hate."

He laughed. "Damn. Why do you hate your own cousin?"

"She made my life a living hell, when we were kids.

We were in the same grade, at the same school. She was like a bloodthirsty Barbie, always teasing me for being a late bloomer and a redhead and for only liking 'boy stuff.' I haven't seen her in ages, but I'm sure she'll be delighted to make an ass of herself, asking how much I love rolling around with other women and pumping iron or whatever."

"Most people get over that dumb kid shit by the time they hit their thirties."

"Don't count on it with her. She's the reason I left Facebook."

He grinned at her, mischievous.

"What?"

"I'll go as your beard."

Steph rolled her eyes, smiling. "I don't need a beard. She's seen me with plenty of guys over the years. That's just the lowest-hanging fruit, my being into manly stuff or whatever. The implication doesn't bother me, and she knows it. It's just shorthand for her saying, 'I'm still the prom queen, and you're still the weirdo jock girl with no boobs.'"

"Maybe she got fat," Patrick offered.

"Not according to her wedding announcement," Steph said with a dramatic, faux-lamenting sigh.

"Ah, a wedding... *The evil bitch cousin's wedding*," he said in a low, gravelly tone fit for a movie trailer.

"It doesn't matter anyway. I don't want to *win*. I just hate that she thinks it's okay to treat me like that."

"You don't have to go to the wedding if you don't want to, right?"

"No, I don't. But I want to see all my other family. And I want to eat crab cakes and drink champagne on her dime."

He laughed.

"And I need to find the perfect dress this week, so I'll look as good as possible while I do it."

As they drove, Steph's thoughts wandered to the looming mixer. Yesterday she'd felt hopeful, but now…dread, more dread. Just as it had soured any feelings she'd kindled for Dr. Dylan, this latest taste of Patrick had spoiled her appetite for other men.

Suck it up, Healy. Stick to the plan.

The sex was clouding her reason. There was a voice in the back of her head, its whispers growing louder. *You like him. More than you've ever liked anybody.*

But I won't have a child, not until the financial uncertainty's passed. If Steph believed in anything, it was preparation. And how long would it take to get to a good place financially with a guy like Patrick? It could be years, and she was thirty. You could gamble on those things when you were twenty-five. You were *immortal* at twenty-five. But something changed at thirty. That nagging voice said, *You've got ten years to realistically make this motherhood thing happen.* Knock off two or three as a relationship was kindled to the point where it might prove to be the right one, another few for a second go-round, should the first effort not pan out. Add a couple more, should a man like Patrick prove himself the one, and they waited to get to a safe place with their finances.

Forty would be here in a blink.

She hated to even be thinking this way, but time was a real factor, in a way it never had been before. She didn't want to go into her next serious relationship with her fingers crossed, breath held, blindly praying that once the initial lust cooled, the foundation she'd discover underneath would be solid enough to build a family on. That connection was key, to be sure, but it wasn't enough. Not without stability.

Her head was spinning.

They reached Lynn, and only took a couple wrong turns before finding Rich's street. "That one, I think," Steph said, pointing to a pale green three-story halfway down the block.

"How will you get home?" Patrick asked.

"I can just hop on the train."

"You sure? I could like, go grab myself a coffee, take you the rest of the way in an hour...?"

She waved the offer away. "No, no. You're way too nice. This is Rich's place—my gigantic Hispanic coworker? He's dating Lindsey, from Spark, and she's looking for a roommate. And I'm looking for an apartment."

"Oh, gotcha."

"So if I like the place, after brunch I'll want to see how far the walk to the station is, see what the neighborhood's like."

"Sounds smart."

"Oh f—" Steph bit her lip, spotting Rich out front, scattering salt on the stoop and sidewalk. He glanced up as Patrick's truck slowed to a stop along the curb. Eyeing Steph through the windshield, he blinked coyly between her and her chauffeur.

"Crap crap crap."

"What?"

She groaned. "I'm never going to hear the end of this—poaching a contractor from work."

Patrick grinned. "Busted."

Rich wandered over and Steph rolled down her window. "Good morning, Rich."

"Morning, Healy. And Patrick, right?"

"Nice to see you again." Patrick opened his door and hopped out to pull Steph's bag from behind the seats. Rich used the opportunity to lean along the open window and mutter, "Electrician, huh? Bow-chicka-wow-wow. Did your pizza boy not arrive within thirty minutes?"

"Ah ha ha ha."

"Does he make house calls?"

"May I please exit?"

Rich stepped back and opened Steph's door as Patrick

brought her bag around. "You into brunch, Patrick?" Rich asked.

Oh Lord.

"My mom's making enough *calentado* to feed the neighborhood."

"I dunno what that is, but I won't say no to anybody's mom's cooking."

"C'mon in, then."

Patrick shot Steph a belated glance and she shrugged to say, *Sure. What the hell?*

Rich tossed the last of a scoop of salt down the sidewalk and led them up the steps.

"Who else is here?" Steph asked.

"Just my mom and sister and Linds." He opened the first door as they entered the building and waved them inside.

They walked into a large kitchen, bustling with good smells and laughing women. Steph and Patrick were introduced to Rich's mother, Lorena, a stout, slow-moving woman with a kind smile and a heavy Colombian accent, and his younger sister, Diana, dressed in scrubs, round face framed in black curls. Steph and Patrick had both met Lindsey already of course, but they shook all the same. Lindsey waited until Patrick was being plied with coffee by their hostess, then sidled up to Steph.

"I didn't miss something, did I? Jenna didn't sign Patrick up for Spark when my back was turned, did she?"

"No. This is all very…unsanctioned."

Lindsey nodded slyly, like they'd just entered into a conspiracy together. "Good work. I had a chance to chat with him when he was doing the lights in the office. He seems really sweet."

"He is."

"And *really* cute."

"Yes, that, too. But it's just casual. Rich caught us pulling up together and invited him."

"Do you wish he hadn't?"

"No, not really. I wasn't looking to get busted and give your boyfriend any more reasons to rib me at work, but since I have…"

"May as well feed the man, right?"

Steph smiled at that. Of course Patrick deserved a bit of the girlfriend treatment, seeing how he'd driven her all the way to Lynn when he could've stayed in his nice warm bed.

She nodded. "May as well."

PATRICK HAD NEVER had Colombian brunch before, but damn—Denny's had nothing on Lorena Estrada. He finished helping load the dishwasher then clutched his belly dramatically, smiling at his hostess. "I think I gained about ten pounds, Lorena. Thanks. That was the best meal I've had in ages."

Though she waved the compliment away, it clearly had her glowing.

Lindsey had taken Steph upstairs to check out the apartment and its spare bedroom, and Rich's sister had left for work. Rich was tidying the table and stowing condiments and spices, and when Patrick was dismissed from any further chores, he headed for the door.

"I'll just head up and see if Steph needs a lift home," he said.

"Before you go." Rich followed Patrick into the empty landing.

"Yeah?" Oh hell, was he about to get grilled by Steph's massive cage-fighter coworker about his intentions toward her? Their brunch-time conversation had told Patrick that he and Rich weren't destined to become bosom friends anytime soon. The guy had a cocky, protective thing going on, and a stare that went cold when he turned his attention to another male.

"You said you used to be a carpenter?" Rich asked.

Patrick's heart resumed beating. "Still am. Restoration stuff."

"Tough market these days, I bet."

"There's an understatement."

Rich's dark eyes shifted. "Lemme quit acting like I got any tact—Steph said you're hurting, work-wise."

"Did she?"

"She didn't say what guy she was talking about at the time, but yeah. She did."

Patrick nodded. "She's not wrong." Steph had talked about him to her friend? What else had she said, he had to wonder.

"I grew up in this house," Rich said, gazing around them. "Same as my little sister. My dad died here."

"Oh, sorry."

Rich waved the apology aside. "It's got my family's entire history in this country, all in these walls, good and bad. I just closed on the building last week."

"Ah. Congrats."

"My mom's lived in this town for over thirty years, and after all that time, she finally doesn't have to answer to a landlord."

Patrick smiled politely to cover his impatience, unsure exactly where this patriarchal lecture was leading, issued by a man likely five years his junior. If it was toward work, he'd let the arrogant shtick slide.

"I could've bought a nicer place," Rich said, "but this was what I wanted. I know the siding needs replacing and the front steps are on borrowed time…"

Patrick cheered, pleased this was heading in a direction that might involve a payday.

"Would you say you're better at carpentry than electrical work?"

Patrick laughed. "Night and day."

Rich gave him a shrewd look.

"You need something done?"

"I know it's nothing special, as architecture goes," Rich continued.

Patrick nodded. It was just another anonymous, mirror-image pair of multi-family homes, slapped together to fill a need and turn a profit. Then he remembered those unique, charming triple-deckers he'd gotten to look inside in Worcester. Basically housing for immigrant workers in the mid-twentieth century, but with so much pride put into the details. He pictured Rich's sagging porches, imagining stained cedar in place of the sad, whitewashed plastic-blend the last carpenter had used. He pictured Lorena's kitchen, and how cheerful it would look with the old re-re-re-painted cabinets ripped out, sunlight gleaming off walnut and glass.

"You've got plenty of potential, if the foundation's solid."

Rich nodded. "Half a quarry's worth of granite."

He crossed his arms. "Are you offering me work?"

Rich glanced into the kitchen, then beckoned Patrick to follow. His mother had finished tidying, leaving the room empty. He gestured for Patrick to sit at the table. "Probably not work in the way you'd prefer." Rich fetched a pair of beers from the fridge.

Patrick politely waved the bottle away. "What way, then?"

"I'm not rolling in liquid assets," Rich said, opening his own beer. "It'd have to be piecemeal, a project at a time, as my fight pay allows. Maybe ten hours a week or so, to start."

"Ten hours is better than nothing."

"Or, I could buy your labor for the cost of rent and utilities—I've got an empty unit on the other side."

Patrick had to laugh. "I believe my great-great-great-grandparents would call that indentured servitude."

Rich grinned and tapped his bottle to Patrick's unopened one. "I won't pretend that as the son of dirt-poor immigrants, I don't find that fact a little bit satisfying. Oh, hey—you know anything about plumbing?"

"I'm *nearly* as good a plumber as I am an electrician," Patrick promised.

"That's terrifying. But every slumlord needs a crooked super, right? What do you think? Too raw a deal?"

Patrick did a little math. The rent on a two-bedroom unit around here was probably fifteen hundred or thereabouts—only as much money as he'd make doing part-time work. Though if he turned his own place into a rental…

It didn't feel right. He shook his head. "Too raw. But I'll take any jobs you've got to offer, as they come. If the price is fair." That was a bit of a bluff—he was so desperate to be doing carpentry again, he'd be tempted by anything over minimum wage, provided it didn't interfere with any other work he might hustle.

Rich nodded, thinking.

"How much creative freedom you offering?" Patrick asked. That would certainly sweeten the deal.

"My mom'll want her say," Rich said. "But as far as I'm concerned, just do a classy job and improve the value of the place, and I'm happy."

Patrick looked around the kitchen. "At ten hours a week, it'll take years to get six units and their decks looking like something special."

"There'll be months when I could buy you out for sixty hours a week," Rich said. "But not consistently. It all depends on my fights, and whether I've got tenants in all the apartments."

Sixty hours a week of pure custom carpentry sounded like heaven to Patrick. Still… "I um, I better ask Steph how she'd feel about it. If she winds up living here, it might be weird to have me hanging around all the time. I've already come on stronger than she's happy about."

Rich smirked. "You putting your chances with a woman over steady work?"

The question threw Patrick, because it nailed exactly what had him hesitating. "Yeah, I suppose I am."

Rich took a deep drink, then stood, giving Patrick a clap on the arm. "Don't feel bad. I'm supposed to be off in California right now, living and breathing my next match. Instead I'm freezing my ass off back home, playing coach and landlord. A woman rewrote my plans, too."

Patrick stood. He offered his hand, met by Rich's firm shake. He wasn't *so* bad, Patrick decided. Probably just out of practice at viewing other men as anything other than opponents. "I'll think about it. And I'll talk to Steph." He pulled a card out of his wallet. "Send me an email with a list of the priority projects you'd like done, and I'll put an estimate together."

"Will do."

They shook again and Patrick showed himself to the landing. He jogged up the steps and found Steph and Lindsey chatting in the third floor apartment. Nice place— sunny and roomy. Prematurely, his carpenter's brain began assembling a list of improvements. He waited until Steph spotted him loitering in the doorway.

"Hey," she said, wandering over. "You heading back north?"

"Only if you're done with me. You need a lift?"

"No, thank you. I'm going to keep grilling Lindsey for a bit, then maybe have a wander around the neighborhood."

"Okay." He hit a standstill, not sure how to say good-bye. He'd have been angling for a kiss, except with Lindsey right there, it felt awkward.

Steph rose on her toes to give him a quick hug, rubbing his back. "Thanks again for the lift. And for dinner," she added more quietly. "And everything."

It wasn't a kiss, to be sure, but as she dropped back, he

felt all warm and squishy nonetheless. "My pleasure. Maybe I'll see you around?"

Her smile tightened. "Maybe."

He stepped forward to shake Lindsey's hand. "Good to see you again. Nice place."

She smiled, blue eyes narrowing with curiosity. Was that a matchmaker's assessing study? Or the look of a woman who'd just been made privy to some pertinent female secrets? "Thanks. Good to see you, too."

"Give my best to Jenna."

"I will. Drive safe."

He cast Steph a final smile, and headed for the stairwell.

Things with her always felt kind of murky and shapeless, so he shrugged the uncertainty off, trying to focus on the job opportunity he'd stumbled into. Whenever he was with her, good stuff just seemed to materialize.

As he trotted down the weathered, creaking front steps, his brain got busy jotting to-dos. He cast the building a backward glance.

It was no craftsman, no colonial, no Tudor revival, to be sure. But with a lot of satisfying work—and a certain redhead's blessing—this place *could* become something really special.

And procuring said redhead's blessing was a fine excuse to make use of her very hard-won phone number in a couple days' time. He smiled at that, feeling warm despite the overcast winter sky.

11

For the next week, Steph tried her damnedest not to think about Patrick.

Just get on with work. Just get her head out of that fog he produced, with that smile and those eyes, and that sense-blocking smokescreen created by the fireworks their bodies made.

Her miracle hadn't arrived at the mixer. *Steph* hadn't even arrived at the mixer. She'd dressed, done her hair, stood by her door for ten minutes or more, fingering her keys. Sex with Patrick had been as sumptuous as Thanksgiving, and now the thought of even *kissing* another guy was about as appealing as soggy saltines.

In the end she'd listened to her gut, and called Jenna to apologize. "I'm just off tonight. I know myself, and going would be a bad idea." She'd stayed in and gorged on two bags of microwave popcorn and a Netflix bender—anything to keep her mind off Patrick.

She was still undecided about Lindsey's apartment. Cute place, decent neighborhood...but all the same faces from work, once she headed home for the night. She needed time to think about it.

On Tuesday she tag-teamed with Rich, joining Mercer for several interviews to find Wilinski's a new general manager. Those duties had fallen to Mercer since the gym's founder, his mentor, had passed away two years earlier, though he claimed he wasn't suited to the gig. He'd much prefer to be training, full-time, and the gym was finally turning enough of a profit that it could afford to hire a proper GM. Hopefully someone who could drag them even further into the black through the magic of clever accounting.

So far the frontrunner was a tiny, soft-spoken twentysomething named Yanlin, who lived across the street with her parents above the little Chinese grocery store they owned. She was a freshly minted CPA, and had glanced at their books and software and offered a bunch of useful cost-cutting suggestions, which excited Mercer. Plus she was web-savvier than the three trainers combined. Steph was dubious of hiring a GM who boasted absolutely *no* working knowledge of the sport, but she didn't argue that Wilinski's could use a studious accountant-type to get the place organized. Someone whose focus wouldn't fall to pieces whenever a big event drew near.

Steph had that Wednesday off. She set out from her apartment just after ten, with a printed map of every store within a five-mile radius that might yield the prize she sought—a kick-ass dress for Kristy's wedding. One that'd make her look like a million bucks. For two hundred dollars or less.

Her hopes were high as the mission began. It was exciting to have an occasion that warranted such a splurge, but she was soon reminded exactly how behind her peers she was when it came to shopping.

She didn't really know what styles flattered her athletic build—and tricked the eye into seeing hips and boobs and a backside where there really weren't any—or what her colors were, or how to accessorize. Salesgirls tried to help, but after hitting four stores in two hours, endlessly changing in and out of dresses and winter layers… Nothing. Not so much as a single viable candidate.

Then in the fifth store, a formalwear boutique, she spotted a gown she liked. A lot.

It was a wedding dress, but the appeal had nothing to do with a desire to rush down the aisle. It was the gown itself, watery-smooth satin, strapless, the fabric gathered elegantly at the bust and falling in silvery cascades from the fitted waist.

It said things to her.

Whispered things, as though it were hell-bent on seducing her.

Clothes never did this to Steph. She got stuck standing there, admiring the gown, touching it fondly, fingering the glimmering embellishments at the center of the bodice.

A salesgirl came over, smiling.

"It's beautiful," Steph said.

"I love that one. So understated. When's the big day?"

She laughed. "It's this weekend. But it's not mine— I'm just a guest. But this one nearly makes me wish I was the bride."

"These can be bridal-party dresses, too. They come in white, then we dye them custom."

Intrigued, Steph flipped the tag over. *Six hundred bucks?* Goddamn. What sick bride would do that to her best friends?

"You've got gorgeous coloring," the girl said, eyes narrowing savvily. "Forgive me for asking, but you're about a four, right?"

Steph nodded, eyes still caught on the gown, despite its ridiculous price tag.

"Hang on one moment." The girl excused herself, disappearing past a velvet curtain. She returned in a moment with a length of satin draped over her arm, the cool, pale gray-blue of winter itself. She unfurled it, revealing the same gorgeous cut as the white dress. "Size four," she explained. "A custom order, but there wound up being a fit issue."

"It's beautiful," Steph said, barely daring to touch it. Even prettier in this color.

"Would you like to try it on?"

She hesitated. "Six hundred is way out of my budget." And it wasn't as though she'd have another excuse to wear a gown for another couple years, at least. If she was even still a four, by then.

"Since it's a sample, it wouldn't be full price. I'd have to talk to my manager, but I bet we could get it down to three fifty."

Yikes. That was still way more than she'd planned on. She'd have to skip the new shoes and get a cheapo haircut to even *begin* to justify it.

"Maybe three hundred," the salesgirl added.

Steph still wasn't sold.

"Just try it on," the girl suggested. "It might give you a sense of what shape you're after."

Steph folded, accepting the cool, slippery dress. "Okay. Trying it on can't hurt."

Only it *did* hurt, because it looked *amazing*. It didn't need a stitch of alteration, sliding over her contours perfectly, even giving her the illusion of a bust and hips—if modest ones—and balancing her strong shoulders. It was fitted around the trunk and made her boobs sort of…float. Like magic. Made her not-quite-green eyes look greener, her hair redder. And the skirt positively slithered around her legs, too, like sex-made-satin. Damn.

But she couldn't blow three hundred bucks on a dress she'd wear for one evening. She wouldn't even have a date to take the thing off her. She wanted to look awesome in front of Kristy, but no matter how potent that petty, irratio-

nal urge was, it wasn't happening at this price. She sighed
and reached back to unzip the gown, wishing she'd never
tried it on. No other dress would ever measure up, now.

She handed it back to the girl with her thanks, wishing the price would magically drop further. But it didn't.

She put it out of her mind and tried the next store. Nothing. She was burning out, all the excitement bled from the
mission. A few hours on, she wound up at a department
store, and found two party dresses in her budget that she
liked. Neither made her feel like the winter-colored gown
had, but they were cute, and fairly flattering—one a blue
strapless style, the other a beaded black number that looked
far more expensive than it was. She was torn.

She aimed her phone at her reflection in the changing
room mirror, and snapped a picture. She hit Share and
typed a text. *Need opinions. Option A?* She cued up her
mom's number, but her finger froze above the send button.
It wasn't a mom's approval she wanted. A mom wouldn't
have Steph's sex appeal in mind. Impulsively, she rewrote
her message. *Got my bitch cousin's wedding this weekend.
What do you think? Option A?* She found Patrick's number,
and sent the photo.

She changed into the blue dress and snapped a second
picture. *Or option B?*

Her phone jingled before she'd even changed back into
her street clothes. She checked the message, heart thumping.

*depends. any single men going to be at this wedding? if
so option c burlap sack*

She laughed, then another message chimed.

*just kidding. i like the blue one. looks pretty with your
hair*

She smiled, something wriggly and pleasant and terrifying upsetting her middle. Suddenly, she didn't care what
Kristy thought about how she looked. It was Patrick she

wanted to wow. Patrick's eyes she wanted assessing her, with that naked hunger glowing behind heavy lids, transforming him into the bossy man she'd met in his bedroom. She pursed her lips and stared at the two dresses hung on the rail. She did some math. No new shoes, and she could skip the cut altogether if she wore her hair up…

The stores would be closing soon.

"Screw it." She abandoned the dresses on the rack outside the changing rooms.

As she marched out the door and back toward the bridal boutique, she scrolled for Patrick's number and hit Talk.

"Steph?"

"Patrick. Hey." Her voice came out huffy and stilted from her hurried pace.

"Uh-oh… Are you pissed, about me saying that thing, about other guys checking you out?"

She laughed. "Of course not. I'm just speed-walking. I'm calling to see if you're free this weekend. And if you'd like to be my date for that wedding."

"Oh."

"It's in Worcester. You'd be meeting my parents and my older brother, and probably staying the night, on my parents' fold-out in the basement. With me. So it's kind of a heavy date, on paper."

"Is it a heavy date in your head?"

"I don't know," she admitted. "And I've decided I don't care."

"Black tie or just a suit?"

"Just a suit," she said, dodging a gaggle of noisy teens.

"I've got one of those. What time do I pick you up?"

She smiled to herself and hauled the door to the bridal shop open. "Two o'clock, Saturday?"

"I'll be there."

They said goodbye, and Steph aimed herself at the salesgirl. Damn, she'd really wanted some new shoes…

"How about two fifty for that pale blue sample gown?" she asked.

The salesgirl made a show of hesitating. She consulted in the back with her manager for an extraordinarily long time while Steph idly tried on tiaras, finally returning with a smile and the perfect dress all zipped up in a garment bag.

"Two fifty," she agreed, "but the sale would be final."

Steph pulled out her wallet. "Deal."

SHE WAS A nervous wreck on Saturday morning, blowing time before Patrick was due to pick her up.

Was she nervous because of him, or about seeing her awful cousin? Was she nervous Kristy would say something nasty, share some embarrassing war story from Steph's adolescence in front of Patrick? Was she nervous her parents wouldn't like him?

Or was she terrified of a much likelier possibility—that they'd *love* him?

Four times she took the dress out of its bag and tried it on. Obsessed over her accessories. Practiced in her heels.

Just after two, she unzipped herself one last time and dressed in street clothes. She'd change and do her hair and makeup at her parents' house.

While Patrick did what? Shot the shit with her dad while the girls got gussied up?

Well, yeah. Probably. They'd find a zillion manly things to talk about. Bruins, Pats, Celtics. Real-estate prices, gas prices, snow-blower engines. Patrick would be fine.

He arrived five minutes early and she met him in the foyer. *Oh dear.*

Oh dear, oh dear. He looked gorgeous.

"Wow." She took in his charcoal suit and the crisp collared shirt that made his crazy-blue eyes even crazier-blue.

"I clean up okay, right?" He smiled and kissed her cheek. "Changing in Worcester, I take it?"

"Yeah." She led them out to his truck. "I paid *way* too much for my dress. No way I'm chancing any wrinkles."

"The blue one, right?" he asked as he opened her door. "That definitely had my vote."

"You'll see."

"It better be. I picked this shirt so we'd match."

She laid the garment bag gently in the back of the cab and set her overnight tote between her feet. They buckled up and hit the road.

Goodness, she was excited. She hadn't been this excited since right before junior prom—the last time she'd had an excuse to wear anything resembling a gown, come to think of it. Her date had been a guy friend, no chance of romance, but she'd still been stoked to feel girly for a night. Then Kristy had ruined everything. Steph had arrived feeling like a movie star, but left convinced her dress had been dated and dumpy, that her hair—which she'd thought looked rather Julia Robertsy—resembled a bad eighties perm, and that her freckled arms and shoulders were an affront to all things feminine and desirable. It had been so dispiriting, she'd skipped her senior prom altogether.

"I can't believe I'm actually looking forward to this," she said as Patrick merged them onto the highway.

"Because of your cousin? She'll be so busy, you could probably just do a half-assed, drive-by congratulations and avoid her the rest of the night."

"Here's hoping. She was so horrible to me my entire childhood."

"Is this some big makeover moment, where you show off how awesome you look, and that you're a celebrity and everything?"

She laughed. "I'm not a celebrity."

"You're in magazines."

"MMA magazines. In sidebars."

"You've got a Wikipedia entry."

She blinked. "Do I?"

"Yup. I bookmarked it. Your little profile picture's bad-ass. You're kicking some blonde chick in the arm."

"Huh. Well, if I'm completely honest, yes, this is a bit of a revenge opportunity."

He shot her a grin.

"What?"

"And you picked me to show off to your cousin, right? Not some fancy guy from Spark?"

"You're more handsome than any guy Jenna's set me up with, and yes, that did factor a bit."

"Nice."

She laughed. "I guess I didn't need to bother worrying you'd feel used."

"You plan on using me for any other purposes, before the night's over?"

She smirked, blushing. "I may."

"Well, I don't know that a woman's ever told me point-blank that she intends to exploit my handsomeness then use me for sex. And I can't say it's leaving me feeling too much of anything aside from smug."

And with that fun tone set for the day, they passed the rest of the drive in easy conversation and singing along to the classic rock station.

They arrived at Steph's childhood home right on time. She hugged her parents and introduced them to Patrick, and just as expected, the men quickly fell into a conversation about some union dispute that had made the news, leaving Steph and her mom to head upstairs and get ready.

"He seems awfully nice," her mother called. She was changing in her bedroom, Steph in the adjoining bathroom.

"He is."

"And awfully handsome."

"He's awfully great in almost every way," Steph assured her, "but we're not a couple or anything. We're just casual."

"What a waste."

Steph smoothed the dress and made her first entrance of the night, eager to draw her mom away from the topic of Patrick's wonderfulness.

"Oh, Penny." Her mom abandoned an effort to clasp her necklace.

"Steph, Mom. Please."

"Sorry, honey. Oh my, you look beautiful."

"You, too."

"Turn," her mom directed, twirling her finger. "Just *look* at that." She descended on the dress, stroking and preening and making Steph swish this way and that. "And all these years I've worried about you breaking your neck… It's almost worth it, for your figure, isn't it?"

They did their makeup and hair in front of the old vanity. Steph slipped into her heels and tossed a compact and lip gloss in the little clutch purse she'd bought, and they met the men downstairs. They hadn't moved from the kitchen, though the conversation had shifted to hockey.

"Well, look at you two!" her dad said, goggling wildly at them.

Patrick didn't say a word, though his eyes spoke volumes. His eyes said things that Steph gladly would have paid two hundred and fifty dollars to hear, things that made her feel at once angelic and devilish.

"I'll fetch your brother," her dad announced. He was already in his usual no-fuss wedding ensemble—khakis, with a sweater vest over a dress shirt. He hadn't bothered with a tie and Steph's mom had long given up trying to force one on him. It lasted about as long as sunglasses on a toddler.

In the few minutes it took her dad to lure Tim out of the apartment above the garage, Steph's mom ascertained half of Patrick's life story and made herself familiar enough to straighten his tie and pick the lint off his shoulders.

"Let's do this thing," Tim said as he entered, dressed in

a button-up and slacks. He stopped short, spotting Patrick.
"Hey, man. Good to see you again. Steph didn't say she was
bringing a date. Not to mention one I'd actually approve of."

They shook and Patrick told Tim how his new timing
belt was faring while everyone got their coats on.

Steph and Patrick took his truck, and her brother rode
with their parents—Tim wasn't the most temperate guy,
and given that this wedding boasted an open bar, he'd be
in no state to drive himself home by the time it was over.

"Still nervous?" Patrick asked Steph, following her parents' old sedan.

"A little."

"I think I passed parental muster, at least."

She smiled. "I was never worried about that. Everyone
seems to love you." A sad pang caught her as she remembered there was one person who hadn't—not for keeps. The
one he'd exchanged vows with.

For rich or for poor.

Had it been gauche to invite him to a wedding? Was a
year long enough to make peace with one's own failed marriage? It only took a glance at that easy smile for Steph to
remind herself this man wasn't the type to begrudge anyone their happiness. Probably didn't know the meaning of
the word *grudge*.

Her heart was pounding with hard, anxious thumps by
the time they arrived at the venue—a country club whose
golf course looked exceedingly majestic, coated in perfect
white snow. The entryway was decorated with cool yellow and orange origami flowers, more of the same leading
them into a big hall, where dozens of chairs faced a stage
draped in white. An official-looking guy was going over a
folder of notes with Steph's cousin Jessie, the bride's older
sister, who looked pretty in her butter-yellow matron-of-
honor gown, her four-year-old son busy yanking at its hem.

The hall was lined with tall windows that looked out

across the course and its pond, and a string quartet stood off to one side, playing upbeat music.

"Slick," Patrick said.

"Yeah, it's beautiful."

Steph had vague visions of her own wedding, but they didn't look a thing like this. At least half her friends were fighters. They'd have much more fun set loose in a state park or at the beach, drinking and joking through a barbecue reception. Steph would, too. But for tonight, dressing up and playing tourist in this kind of elegant affair was fun.

They found Steph's parents and Tim, and her older brother Robbie was there as well. He'd dressed a bit sharper than the other Healy men, in a black suit. He'd had a rough early adulthood—too much partying, a few legal scrapes. But since he'd quit drinking five years earlier, he'd pulled himself together. He'd earned an associate's degree and was nearly through his certification to become a licensed social worker. Sobriety suited him. Steph found it difficult to even recall the old Robbie.

They hugged, and she introduced him to Patrick. Robbie wasn't as chatty as their parents or Tim; more sensitive, more of an observer. He'd be watching his little sister's date as the night went on, she knew, and carefully weighing his verdict.

"Damn, girl," he said as he stepped back from a second hug. "Where'd my tomboy sister go, huh?"

"She retired," Steph said. "Well, no. She hasn't. But she's clocked out for the weekend."

"You look great. Haven't seen you all dressed up like this since your prom night."

She blushed at that. "Don't remind me."

"Why not? You were a knockout then, too."

"I was?" Maybe Kristy had only brainwashed her into thinking she'd looked awful.

"Yeah. You wouldn't believe the limbs I threatened to break if your date tried anything with you."

She laughed. That did sound like the old hothead Robbie—the type to get all macho on a guy who looked at his baby sister funny. Who'd embodied the myth of the bad-tempered redhead.

"I could've handled that myself," she said.

Patrick looked between them. "I feel like maybe I should have worn some padding under this suit."

Robbie pretended to eyeball him with suspicion. "Just keep your nose clean, Doherty, and we won't have any trouble."

People began arriving in earnest and the music changed, the quartet switching to more ceremonial-sounding tunes.

"Big wedding," Patrick said as they edged their way down a row of seats, following Steph's parents.

"I know. Nearly two hundred guests."

"With an open bar? Damn."

"Her fiancé's some kind of banker or investor or something. I've never met him. I haven't even seen my cousin in person in at least five years. Not since her sister's wedding." As best she'd gathered, Kristy's betrothed was older, and presumably divorced. Before she'd fled Facebook, Steph had seen the smiley pictures of the happy couple, along with two small children she assumed must be the groom's. He'd looked kind of schmoozy and obnoxious in those shots, with slicked-back hair and a gold earring. The kind of banker who rode an oversize, noisy Harley on the weekend, she'd decided. Kristy was welcome to him.

Damn, she really had to quit with the petty thoughts.

The procession began—a collection of people Steph had never met coming down the aisle, her cousin Jessie and some other bridal-party members; her Aunt Pam; her cousin's soon-to-be stepsons in miniature suits, corralled by their father. The room collectively giggled and *aww*ed each time he had to aim one of them in the right direction. Steph didn't get a good look at him until he reached the stage and turned, the children taken in hand by an older woman—their grandmother, likely. The groom looked nervous and excited, fidgeting beside the officiant. He wasn't the slick operator Steph had pegged him as—just a father approaching forty, with a nice smile, a touch heavy but carrying it well. Finally came the bride and Steph's uncle John, and everyone swiveled in their seats to murmur and snap photos.

Kristy looked beautiful.

She wasn't as beautiful as she had been in high school— her looks had an expiration date, not aided by her tanning regimen. As a teenager she'd been a knockout, but at thirty she'd settled into a less dazzling persuasion of pretty. But she had something going for her now that she'd lacked at eighteen—she looked *happy.*

She was smiling in a way Steph had never seen. Nothing tight or staged about it. And that made her more beautiful than she'd ever been as homecoming queen. Steph didn't even notice the details of her dress until she was standing before her groom—that smile eclipsed everything else.

The ceremony was brief and sweet, and before Steph knew it, everyone was filtering out in the happy couple's wake, bound for the ballroom where dinner and dancing and drinking would take place.

Patrick grabbed her hand as they shuffled toward the hall. Whether he was worried about losing her or simply hoping to use that as an excuse to hold her hand…she found she didn't care.

There was much milling and queuing for the bar, a thousand micro-reunions happening all around them. Steph and Patrick got drinks and found their table, a wide one with the Healys plus a random assortment of distant cousins. A waiter came around to address their empty champagne flutes. Robbie flipped his upside down before it could be filled, smiling politely.

Steph drank her merlot a bit too quickly, steeling herself for the inevitable. She kept her eyes on the mingling bride, and when the crowd around Kristy began to thin, she looked to her parents, then Patrick. "Shall we say congrats?"

"You two go," her mom said, busy dabbing at her husband's vest. "Your father's just spilled beer all over himself."

Shoot—no chance at diluting this encounter with a wall of family. Tim was nowhere to be found, and when she looked beseechingly to Robbie he just grinned and sipped his iced tea, that cool look telling her, *Get your big-girl pants on and bite the bullet.*

Fine. She took Patrick's arm and they got up, dodging servers.

Her heart thudded harder with every step that brought them closer to the bride and groom. What on earth was she afraid of, anyway? It wasn't like Kristy would say anything nasty to her—not with so many witnesses. *Not with her mouth, she won't.* But those eyes. One judgmental sweep of those eyes and Steph could be left doubting herself the rest of the night. Ridiculous what that woman could do, when Steph stared down far tougher chicks in the ring. *Tougher,* she thought. *But not half as mean.*

The groom was busy chatting when an opening appeared before Kristy. Her eyes locked on Steph's with surprise and a smile overtook her face.

"Penny!"

No use correcting her—the last time they'd spoken, that had still been her name.

"Hey, Kristy. You look amazing. Congratulations." She hazarded a hug that was accepted warmly.

"You look…" Kristy took her in, freezing Steph's blood in her veins. "You look… Wow. You look so grown up."

"Oh. Thanks. This is my date, Patrick."

They shook and Patrick lavished the bride with the requisite amount of flattery.

"Well, isn't he a handsome one?" Kristy said to Steph, smiling sideways to tease Patrick.

Yes, yes he is. Suck on it.

"Are you still doing that fighting stuff? I always forget what it's called."

That fighting stuff? Steph stifled a grimace. "MMA. I'm retired from competing, but yeah, I'm a trainer now."

"I told my Brad all about it. He just about died. Brad, honey!" Kristy interrupted the man's conversation, clearly eager to make the belittlement of Steph's sport a group affair. "This is my cousin, Penny! The one we talked about."

Brad's face lit up like a kid meeting Santa. "Penny Healy!"

"Nice to meet you, Brad. Congratu—"

He grabbed her hand, pumping it vigorously. "Oh my God, this is so cool! I saw your last fight, against Kim Lacosta. That was nuts! Are you really retired, now?"

Steph could only blink for a moment. "I am, yeah. Bummer I had to go out on a loss."

Brad waved the thought away. "That roundhouse you got her with, right at the start of the second round? Amazing."

Steph felt herself blushing beet-red. She stole a glance at her cousin. Funny, but that wasn't the grin of a cruel teenage girl, pleased to have embarrassed Steph in front of the cool crowd. That was the grin of a grown woman, genuinely delighted by how excited her new husband was, meeting her cousin. Would wonders never cease?

"Is it true you train in the same gym as Rich Estrada?" Brad asked earnestly. And for ten minutes or more, Steph felt damn-near famous, all her assumptions about this guy flipped inside-out. He was a certifiable MMA nut. By the time people were taking their seats for dinner, she'd invited him to come by Wilinski's some weekend for a free session. Brad accepted, beaming like she'd offered him tickets to the Super Bowl.

"That is too funny," Patrick muttered as they made their way back to their table.

"I know."

He pulled her chair out for her. "And here you were, worried she'd be a jerk to you."

"I guess marrying a guy with such good taste in spectator sports has changed her mind about me," she said, faking arrogance.

The toasts went down free of any drunken best-man drama, and dinner service began. When she RSVPed, Steph had assumed her not-yet-procured date would be the steak type, but one look at the envious way Patrick ogled her scallops and she had to swap. His eyes rolled up with rapture every time he tasted one.

"Good?" she asked.

He groaned. "Amazing. Must be like, an entire stick of butter in these. I hope you dance. I'll need to work this off."

"I wouldn't say I dance well, but I enjoy the hell out of trying."

"Perfect."

The floor filled up almost immediately once dinner was cleared and the spotlight slow dances wrapped. A DJ had taken the place of the quartet, and the younger generation crammed onto the hardwood to get sweaty to the pop music, the older folks migrating toward the bar.

Patrick danced pretty well for a tall guy. He ditched his jacket in no time, rolling his sleeves up to his elbows, face aglow with the exertion. Steph felt aglow from the big, warm hand on her waist during the slow numbers, his thrilling heat seeping straight through the satin, through her skin, right into her bones. He was the best-looking man in the room, she decided, holding him close, swaying to the music. When she stole a glance at his face, she could see dark promises in his eyes. His hand tightened at her waist, telling her, *I know what you like. And I know I can give it to you.*

They must have danced nonstop for a full hour before Steph finally begged for a break—these heels were killers. Patrick met her back at the table after fetching her a fresh glass of wine. Stuck driving, he was still nursing his first one.

Steph kicked her shoes off under the table and flexed her feet. "This has been really, really fun."

"Yeah, it has."

She tossed her head back and sighed her relief for all the world to hear. She met Patrick's eyes squarely, letting him see her with all her defenses down, just a happy, tired woman, exhausted from dancing and laughing. His stare worked its usual magic, though, and her fatigue was forgotten in a breath. All she could think was, *I can't wait to be alone with you again.* And if they left soon, they'd have the house to themselves for a little while.

"Hope you're not all danced out," Patrick said. "I've still got a few songs in me."

"Actually, I was thinking maybe we could skip all the cake-cutting and bouquet stuff. Maybe sneak out? Before my folks do...?"

His brows rose innocently. "What on earth are you suggesting, Penny?"

"You'll find out, if you promise never to call me Penny ever again."

He laughed. "Promise."

"After one more dance."

They stood, carrying their glasses. Steph left her shoes behind—half the women on the dance floor had done the same.

"Whatever you're suggesting," Patrick said, "I hope it's

not anything that'll have your older brother breaking my legs."

"You'll just have to wait and—"

He interrupted her, stopping short and holding up a finger. He fished his blinking phone from his jacket pocket and scanned the screen. "Aw, crap."

"What is it?"

"Sorry. It's my cousin. I have to get this—it could mean work."

"By all means." She took his glass and waved him away toward the quieter side of the room, then watched as he took the call. His face went from nervous to pensive to intrigued, and he was nodding by the time he hung up. His shoulders rose and fell with a gruff sigh. *Bad news.*

She frowned as he walked back to her. "Not work, to judge by your face," she said, handing his drink over.

"Could be, actually. If I show up on this site in Danvers, I could wind up with a couple weeks' contract, wiring an office building."

"Hey, that's great!"

He smiled tightly.

"What's wrong? Are you bummed it's not carpentry?"

He shook his head. "I've got to be there at six tomorrow morning. I'd have to leave. Right now."

She'd never seen so much emotional pain in a man's eyes, and that was saying something—fighters could be real wrecks.

He took her hand. "I'm really, really sorry."

She shook her head, smiling. "Why are you sorry?"

"To leave you here, in the middle of a wedding with no date."

She laughed. "Oh God, that's fine. So I miss one last dance." And another night of mind-blowing sex. "So what?"

"I know this meant a lot to you."

"It did, but it's been a perfect night. It's okay if you need to go now, I swear." She squeezed his fingers. "This is more important. I get it."

He took a deep breath. "You've got to know, there's nothing I'd rather do than be with you here, with your family. And be with you tonight, just us. And wake up with you tomorrow."

All at once, her eyes stung.

Whoa.

Steph only ever cried after matches, overcome by frustration or relief or physical pain. What Patrick was saying didn't even hurt. She might be disappointed, but these words made her feel *wonderful*. She couldn't let him see it—he'd feel even worse if he thought she was upset.

"Seriously, don't worry about it. Work comes first for you right now. And if for some reason you insisted on staying, I'd force you to go."

"I don't want you to think you're less important."

She laughed again. "Right now, I kind of should be. It's *fine.*"

"I don't…I don't want to mess up my chance with you, letting you think you come second."

That one landed like a sock in the gut. This man… He was simply too lovely to be real.

She touched his arm. "You're not. Doing what you need to only makes me think more highly of you. Okay?"

His lips quirked in a limp smile, and he nodded, letting her hand go. "Okay. I'm still sorry though."

"I'm sorry, too, but I've had a great time. You were the perfect date."

"And you'll be able to figure out a ride back tomorrow? Or should I come pick you up, after I finish on site…?"

"No, no. Don't be ridiculous. I already know how I'm getting home, anyhow—I'll ask my dad for a lift to the commuter rail, then we'll argue for twenty minutes until I agree to let him drive me all the way to Boston."

He smiled a little easier at that and handed her his glass. "All right. Well, thanks again for inviting me. Your family's great. And tell the bride she looked beautiful, and that those were the best scallops I've ever had."

"I will." Encumbered by the two glasses, she could only passively accept the kiss he leaned in to plant on her cheek. Just the contact of his nose at her temple felt so sweet and familiar that dangerous emotion was welling all over.

"Drive safe," she said as he pulled away. "And good luck with the job."

"Thanks. I'll need it." A final smile, and he was gone, leaving Steph's body suspended somewhere between warm and cold, infatuated and abandoned. She felt tired, suddenly, but the undertone of drunken giddiness… That was all Patrick. He left a little hangover in his wake, a faint ache in her body, with his so far away.

Of all people to bear witness, Kristy came trotting over, smiling broadly, hoisting her gown to keep from tripping. The woman seriously had some kind of radar, designed to hone in on Steph when she felt the most vulnerable.

"Penny! Your date isn't leaving, is he?" Her perky smile drooped dramatically.

"He had a sort of work emergency." *Don't ask what he does.* Steph didn't give a shit about how an electrician stacked up against a banker…but she worried one snide comment from Kristy might have her second-guessing that certainty.

"That's too bad."

"You having a good time on your big day?" Steph asked limply, and added, "You look gorgeous. Patrick said so, too." Her cousin's face was alight from the dancing, some of that teenage beauty shining through.

Kristy shrugged the compliment away, the gesture looking uncharacteristically genuine. "You have no idea how excited I am that this is over—I swear I haven't eaten a

single carbohydrate in three months to fit into this thing."
She smoothed the dress along her waist.

Steph had to smile at that. "I feel your pain. Sounds like
a weigh-in."

Kristy gave Steph an appreciative glance. "What I'd give
for your body, Pen."

Steph laughed, shocked. This from the woman who'd
made her feel like a musclebound freak since puberty.
"Really?"

Kristy sank into a stray chair with a sigh, and Steph followed suit, abandoning the glasses.

"I remember when we were kids, and we'd go to the
lake," Kristy said. She crossed her legs, revealing that she'd
ditched her heels. A Band-Aid decorated her instep, under-
mining her usual vibe of effortless glamour. "You could
just strip down to your swimsuit like it was the easiest
thing in the world."

Steph frowned. She remembered those summer days
differently. Of Kristy sprawled all golden on the sand, tanning beside some bitch friend or other, her imperial expression condemning Steph's pasty, boobless frame or the
racket she and their guy-cousins made, shoving one another off the dock.

"You had the most amazing body," Kristy said. "And you
could eat whatever you wanted. I was so jealous."

"You were? But you were, like, high school royalty."

"I guess. But do you have any idea how hard I had to
work at it? I didn't let myself eat, like, a single gram of
fat, from twelve to twenty-five. Every day, frigging carrot
sticks and diet soda. And there you were, scarfing pizza
like all the guys, actually at peace with your body. While
I was constantly battling mine."

Steph blinked, blindsided. All those mean snipes about
her build, the way she ate... She wanted to ask about those,
but now wasn't the time. Plus it suddenly seemed possible

that those comments had been as reactionary and thought-less as a defensive jab Steph might toss out to keep an op-ponent at bay. Maybe Kristy had barely even registered *saying* those things—words that had echoed in Steph's head for years…

Just as Steph had never realized that her body or her eating habits had struck Kristy like a low-blow, and con-tributed to her own high-school hell.

"I never realized you… I dunno. That you were inse-cure."

Kristy laughed. "No? I thought everyone could tell."

"You were popular. You had it made."

Kristy snorted. "Did your mom never mention all the therapy I had to go through, when we were teenagers?"

"What? No."

"I must have seen about five shrinks. For eating disor-ders and college application stress… I was a *mess*. Mean-while, there you were, actually enjoying the so-called best years of our lives. I'd watch you, around school. With your tiny waist and, like, no body fat, looking all perfect in those skinny-strapped tank tops and track pants that were in. Just joking around with boys like it was nothing."

"Jeez. I always looked at you like… I dunno. Like you knew how to be a girl or something. Like you were in on the secret."

Someone called Kristy's name and she gave them a wave of acknowledgment. As she got to her feet she said, "If I did, the secret must've been, 'treat your body like the enemy.'"

Steph stood. "That's so sad. I had no idea."

"I hated high school. I hated college, too. I switched ma-jors three times while you were in, like, Australia and Japan and all these interesting places. You always knew exactly who you were. I didn't feel that until about three years ago."

"You seem happy now."

She smiled. "I am. Meeting Brad and the boys put stuff

in perspective. Them, and my latest therapist," she said with a guilty smile. "Plus Brad met me when I was feeling really chubby and awful, but the way he looked at me… He saw something in there, I guess. Something underneath. And it made me want to be able to see that, too."

Steph's lips pursed and trembled. Her cousin had made her cry before, but never like this. She got ahold of herself. "Sounds like true love."

Kristy nodded and glanced across the room. "I think they want me for photos. But I'm glad we got to catch up."

"Me, too."

And for the first time ever, not forced by the expectant eyes of family, they hugged.

With a few final volleyed compliments, Steph wished her cousin well.

She found her parents and explained Patrick's disappearance, then spent the rest of the reception camped contentedly at a quieter table with Robbie. When the bride and groom returned to the dance floor, Steph realized with a deep sense of calm that all that old angst was gone, outgrown and cast aside just like Kristy's sharp edges. Funny how love and parenthood did that to people, melted all their prickles away in the face of something so…primal.

Patrick had done that to her. Dissolved her determination to choose with her head, hijacking her sense with the mere nearness of his body, the warmth of his smile. It was too soon to be love though. And her misgivings still lingered.

"Jesus," Robbie muttered. "Tim's wasted."

Steph watched their little brother, dancing as though he were in the grips of a seizure. "That he is."

"Scares the shit out of me," Robbie said. "Thinking he's heading down the same path I took."

"He's had his job over a year now."

"Yeah, that's true…I still worry, though. Thank God

one of us was born with self-control, huh?" He shot Steph a look. "You always had that. Discipline."

She smiled. "I'm just stubborn."

"Whatever it is, keep it up."

They sat in easy silence for a long time, until Robbie said, "Too bad Patrick had to go."

She nodded.

"You said you guys are just casual?"

"Yeah. That's all it really can be, I think." Though it made her heart ache to say so.

"How come?"

"He's so unstable financially. He's on the brink of losing his house."

"That sucks."

"It does, yeah. It's a beautiful little place, and he put a ton of work into it."

"Why can't you date him, though?"

She eyed her brother. "You know how Mom and Dad were, all those years when we were still at home?"

"All the money stress?"

"I lived through that once. I don't think I can handle signing up to go through it again, with a partner."

"He's crazy about you," Robbie said with a smile.

"I'm a little crazy about him, too," she admitted, and felt fresh tears stinging.

"He stares at you like you're cut out of diamond."

Embarrassed, she looked to her hands, fidgeting with her empty wineglass.

"You've dated some real dopes before."

"Thanks for reminding me."

"But some okay guys, too…but none who looked at you like that."

It gave her pause. "No, probably not."

"This one might be down on his luck, but nine guys out

of ten wouldn't find the strength to put aside all this fun on the off-chance they might be able to secure some work."

"He's awfully desperate for it."

Robbie nudged her. "Maybe he's determined. Maybe he's a man who, no matter how rough things got…he'd do what it took to keep the boat afloat."

She stared at her glass. Robbie had a point. Patrick knew what he loved doing, what he was meant to do…but he didn't put himself above a second vocation, not even one that dropped him in a position where he felt incompetent. That had to be humbling. Steph wasn't sure she could do it, herself.

"That was one thing Dad never did," Robbie said quietly. "He never adapted. He never got over thinking he was too good to take any old job to keep the money coming in, even after his skills were basically extinct."

"I hadn't thought about it like that."

"That guy you were dancing with tonight," her brother said slowly. "I can't say I know him, but I had a chance to talk to him. I can tell you a few things."

"Like?"

"I bet he'd take a gig waiting tables at a mall Chili's before he'd roll over and give up the house he loves."

She nodded. "He would." He'd likely be awful at it, mess up orders and drop drinks and get bitched out by jerky customers, but he'd smile through every minute, because that's who Patrick was.

"I'm gonna hit way below the belt and make this about fighting," Robbie warned.

She sighed. "Go ahead."

"You've gone into matches where you said that the other girl was just out of your league, that you *knew* you'd lose."

"And I was usually right."

"But you fought anyway. You knew you'd lose but you

still kept on swinging until you were what, knocked out? About to get an arm broken?"

She nodded.

"That's probably what your friend's feeling these days. He's like, staggering around, bleeding from the head, but he's not gonna stop swinging as long as there's *any* chance that house could stay his."

"No, he's not." Selling the place would make Patrick's life easier...but it wouldn't make him happy.

Meeting some well-off guy might make Steph's life easier.

But could it ever make her happy?

She eyed her parents, sitting at a table closer to the action. Her mom had her hand on her dad's back, rubbing slowly. How many nights had Steph peeked from the dark hallway, watched the two of them sitting just this way at the kitchen table.

All that stress. All those bills. All that misery.

She watched her mom's hand, circling, circling.

And it occurred to her for the first time, that wasn't consolation, that gesture. There was a promise in that contact, one that said, *I'm here, and I'm not going anywhere.* She could have. She could have taken her kids and gone off in search of greener pastures, but she never had. She hadn't run from the struggle. She'd joined the fight and never looked back.

When the going got tough for my parents, Steph realized, *the team got tighter.* The team hadn't disbanded, with one member giving up just because the outcome had grown bleak. Theirs was no fair-weather marriage, as it seemed Patrick's had been.

So what was Steph guilty of? Of not even daring to join Patrick's side, knowing they were doomed to be underdogs for the long haul?

What good is a guaranteed win, she wondered, imagining a stable, comfortable life with some man like Dylan Benedetti, *if you have no passion?* No struggle to keep you hopeful, no loyalty to the ones who shared that struggle?

Robbie nudged her again until she met his eyes. "Guy like that could maybe use a good corner."

She pursed her lips.

"You like him, kiddo. I can tell. And this guy deserves it, unlike some of those losers you used to moon over."

She laughed.

"Do something crazy, Steph."

"Like what?"

"Move in with him. Help him with the mortgage. Dive into the deep end and paddle with him, and see if maybe the struggle doesn't suck so much, if the company's great."

Her heart was pounding, adrenaline pumping through her veins. "That's such a scary leap to take."

Robbie leaned back in his seat, shrugging with a derisive sort of look on his face.

"What?"

"If you don't believe in the guy, then you've got your answer. But I don't think I've ever seen you look at a man like that. Not one I actually approve of." After a brief silence, he drained his iced tea and stood. He cast her a final glance. "And I don't think I've ever known my little sister to give up, just because somebody convinced her she was fighting a losing battle."

She glared at the cheap shot, but her heart wasn't in it. Robbie disappeared into the crowd, leaving her alone with far too many questions.

12

Patrick got home from Worcester just past midnight, yawning mightily. Funny how he'd gone from happy and relaxed to feeling about a hundred years old, all in one drive.

Inside, he bumped the thermostat up to fifty-five, brushed his teeth, stripped to his boxers and set his alarm. His sheets were freezing as he slipped between them. And empty. Funny he would notice—he'd been climbing into this bed alone for over a year now. Except for that one miraculous night, last week.

Man, this sucked. He stared at the ceiling, thinking he ought to be with Steph now, maybe having that awesome, fraught, silent-sex, the kind you have when you're staying at someone's parents' place. That'd probably be hard for her, she was so… Whatever the right word was. Demanding? Physical? Something. The sex probably would have been even hotter for it, with her all frustrated and pent up, trying to be quiet. He smiled at that.

Okay, so not being in the middle of having hot sex with Steph sucked, but on the bright side, maybe he'd score some work in a few hours. Electrical work, but still.

He had that stuff on the horizon for Steph's scary coworker, what's-his-name. Not the most glamorous gig, but it'd be satisfying to take that old three-decker and slowly turn it into something special. Plus maybe Steph would wind up living there, and even if he bungled everything with her this go-around, in a few months they might have some new chances to cross paths. Provided he didn't get all distracted and clumsy and set her unit on fire by mistake.

Fall asleep, he commanded himself. How many hours until he had to be back on the road? Four and a half? Damn, he better get this job. What a kick in the nuts that would be, to miss out on a job *and* the hot sex.

Sleep seemed determined not to come. After twenty minutes of just lying in the dark, he switched on the bedside lamp and propped an extra pillow under his head. His history-buff sister had sent him a massively boring book about Irish genealogy. He opened it to where he'd left off, skimming until he tripped over the surname of a friend or relative.

His eyes opened at the sound of a bell. The book was flopped on his chest and the clock read one-sixteen. Another ring woke him fully, and he tossed the book aside and abandoned the warmth of his bed, jogging through the den. At this hour, an emergency was the most logical explanation, followed swiftly by a very forthright burglar.

He opened his front door, finding neither of those things. He squinted against the glare of the headlights silhouetting Steph. Her gown fluttered in the wind.

"Whoa." He shielded his eyes.

"Hey." What she made of his near nakedness, he couldn't tell—her face was all in shadows. "Can I come in?"

"Of course. Hi."

She waved to the car and someone waved back, then it reversed onto the street.

Patrick closed the door behind her, eyes adjusting. "Wasn't expecting to see you again, tonight."

She smiled. "I'm sorry. You probably need your sleep."

He dismissed the thought with a shrug, then rubbed his goosebumpy arms. "Can we talk in bed? I'm freezing."

"Lead the way."

Once he was settled under the covers, Steph sitting atop them cross-legged in her party ensemble, he had to grin. She'd come all the way here, this late. Somehow. For something.

"Who drove you?"

"My brother. The sober one."

"That was nice of him."

She nodded.

"So what's up?"

"I needed to come and see you. And…and be with you."

Damn. The woman he was nuts about had come all the way from Worcester to be with him? "That's awesome. C'mere."

He tossed the covers aside and she scooted beneath them, curling her body against his. The fabric of her dress felt cool and slippery against his bare skin. She stroked his chest, and he toyed with the hair that had slipped out of her updo, breathed in her exotic perfume smell.

"What'd I do to deserve this long-distance booty call?" he teased.

"You left the party." She met his eyes, expression serious.

"I didn't want to."

"I know you didn't. I know there was probably no other place you wanted to be besides there, with me."

He smiled, bashful. "I told you as much. I'm no good at keeping my feelings a secret."

"But you put work first, and you left."

Was she trying to make him feel bad? Patrick was no good with these sorts of layered conversations.

"You'd do anything you had to, to keep this house."

"Short of hurting somebody or decimating my credit?

Yeah. I would. I think your coworker might have some work for me, actually. Carpentry, on his place in Lynn."

"You'd do whatever it took," Steph reiterated, not seeming to have heard him. "You'd go out and find a job doing anything you could, to make ends meet."

He shrugged and smoothed her hair behind her ear. "Man's gotta do whatever it takes."

"But not every man does."

"I suppose not. But I wasn't raised that way."

She shifted in his arms and met his eyes. "You're a good man. One of the best I've ever met."

He felt himself blushing. "Yeah?"

Her gaze followed her hands as she stroked his neck, his shoulder, chest, belly. He felt the bright heat of flattery first, then something else—something dark and wonderful.

He grinned. "You here to reward me for being such a stand-up guy?"

"I may be."

He pulled the extra pillow out from under his head and tossed it aside, urging Steph onto her back and straddling her. "Is this some new level we're at, where the sex is going to be all sweet and tender? Or do you still like it rough and messy? 'Cause I can swing either way."

"Rough and messy, please."

His cock roused at that, going from curious to hungry in a heartbeat. "You got it."

He rummaged in the side-table drawer for a condom and set it aside. Moving his knees between hers, he eased the hem of her dress up her hips, one slow inch at a time.

"Man, you're gorgeous." He ran the back of his hand along the soft skin of her inner thigh.

She tugged at his arms, biting her lip with impatience.

He laughed. "And you make me feel objectified in the best way." He pushed his shorts down and kicked them away, then eyed Steph's nude panties.

"Uh…better not rip those," she said. "They cost an embarrassing amount."

He laughed, stripping them carefully. Steph was ready with the condom, rolling it down his erection with a smooth motion. Goddamn, he could get used to this woman.

"You need anything first?" he asked, stroking her folds, finding her wet.

"Just you. Now."

The way she held his arms, he knew what she needed. He pushed his hips forcefully between her legs, and entered her with one swift, deep push.

Her fingers curled into claws as she moaned, eyes closing. "Good."

For a thrilling minute he owned her with quick, bossy thrusts, then flipped them over, seating her tightly atop him. She reached back for the zipper, then peeled her dress away. He urged her hips with his hands, loving her weight on him. She worked to take the orders he issued, her body giving him a hundred tiny signals to say she reveled in this treatment. He made his grip meaner, pleased when her lips parted in unmistakable excitement.

"Ride me."

She took him rougher.

"Faster."

She took that command as well, and he thrust from below, intensifying the impact. Bracing her hands on his shoulders, she showed him exactly what her extraordinary body could do.

He kept the act up for as long as he could manage, until excitement stole the control from his muscles, his cock begging for relief, leaving the rest of him overheated and frantic.

It was a race now, and he had to work fast. With her in charge of the motions, he slipped his hand between them, rubbing her clit. That fascinating, strong frame tensed, melting on the next inhalation. Arousal had made a mess of his own body, but he could keep his role up with words, at least.

"Harder. Ride my cock." He hoped he sounded mean— he felt helpless. The best kind of helpless, like the need to come was the cruelest bully, taunting and torturing. He licked his fingers to make them slick, and rubbed her quicker.

"Come for me," he said.

He saw the shift in her as she abandoned the submissive act to chase her pleasure. She rode him in short, rough thrusts, clit seeking the friction of his fingertips.

He said it again. "Come for me. Right on my cock."

And she did. The orgasm had her locked arms shaking, her hips pummeling. It shut her eyes and dropped her mouth open, made her face look mean and needy and gorgeous and electrified.

"Good," he muttered, lost in awe. He could feel her pleasure, a real and physical thing like a fist, squeezing him, pulsing, fluttering. He didn't think he'd ever felt so big. Or so desired.

It was that last one that did him in. The second her eyes opened he flipped them over, rushing after his own orgasm with a flurry of graceless thrusts.

"Oh. Steph." He pushed deep, as deep as he could go, and got lost in the perfect bliss of release for an ageless moment. Dropping to his elbows, he pressed his forehead to hers, rubbed their noses together. He laughed—from the pure joy of their physical connection.

The mania lifted like steam, and behind it was nothing but perfect calm and relief. Once the condom was stripped, he collapsed beside her with a happy, exhausted huff.

She turned to stroke his chest. "Good?"

"Amazing. It always is, with you." He smirked at her.

"That wasn't my best, just now. You had me too wound up to be Mr. Rough-You-Up."

"It was perfect."

He smirked at her. "You're sorta kinky."

A guilty grin. "Just a little."

"I like it. It's fun."

She laughed. "Oh good. Get used to it."

His smile waned then. He wished he *could* get used to it—long-term. But surely she only meant for some finite time being. Still, he wouldn't let it spoil the moment, or the evening. He shifted and locked their legs together, wishing he could trap her here forever, just like this. But surely if anyone could foil such a strategy, it was a pro fighter.

For now, though, she seemed content to be pinned.

They lay in lazy silence as their breathing slowed.

"I'm glad you came over," he murmured, mussing her hair.

"Me, too."

"You and your brother must be close, for him to drive you all the way here so late. Tell him if he ever needs any odd jobs done, I'm at his command."

"I um… I had a talk with him tonight."

"About?"

"About all this stuff, about not knowing what to do about you and me."

"What to do about us…?"

"He told me some things that I don't know if I totally trust, yet, but that I really *want* to be true. About how if two people are right for each other, then they just have to go for it. Just sign up for the hard stuff, and everything will eventually work out."

"Right." This was headed someplace good, wasn't it? He thought so. His pulse beat hard, throat suddenly tight. He took one of Steph's hands, rubbing her knuckles with his thumb.

"I think maybe…I think maybe you're right, for me," she said quietly.

He held her gaze, heart thumping madly as he waited to hear what was coming next.

"I'd like to find out, anyhow."

He squeezed her hand. "I'd like that, too."

"And my entire family and half the gym seem to agree, so maybe I was being stubborn."

"Or scared," he offered. "Your reservations weren't exactly unfounded. I *will* make a pretty shitty suitor, for the foreseeable future. I can't take you anywhere nice, or buy you something decent for Valentine's Day."

"I don't care. I have fun with you. Tonight, dancing. At my neighbor's silly wine-and-cheese thing. Just driving. And, you know." She smiled guiltily. "In bed."

He squeezed her hand again, returning the smile. "Well, if you can suffer the lack of glamour, I'd love for you to take a chance on me."

For a long moment, she didn't speak. He could sense words lurking just behind her lips, and waited for them to reveal themselves. When they did, her thoughts came out in a great crashing wave.

"How would you feel if I moved in with you?"

He blinked. "If you moved in…?"

"I know it's all backward. And rushed. But if I'm going to take a chance, I may as well take a big one."

"I—"

"I could kick in eight hundred a month. That's how much I was budgeting for my rent. Maybe a little more. I'd have to sit down and do some math."

Wait. So. An extra eight hundred bucks a month…and all he had to do for it was sleep in the same bed with Steph every night?

"That'd be amazing. That'd mean… That'd mean I could keep the frigging heat on during the day. And get my truck serviced properly, instead of praying it won't just fall apart before my next job materializes."

She smiled, face full of hope.

"You sure?" he asked. "This doesn't seem like you. A few weeks ago you wouldn't even go on a date with me. You aren't wasted, are you?"

Her grin deepened. "What can I say? You wore me down. Plus you're really good at sex."

"What about your dream man? Those fancy guys you had your heart set on?"

"My brain, not my heart. My heart knew what it wanted the second I laid eyes on you…or the day after, anyhow. Once the swelling went down."

He laughed. "You move here, you'll have a long commute."

She shrugged. "I can read on the train. I've been meaning to do more of that."

"You might wind up hating me."

"And vice versa. But without a lease binding us together, what's the danger?"

"You might wind up loving me?"

Her smile turned softer, and she brushed her lips against his. "Wouldn't that be nice?" For a long time he simply held her, lightly drawing his nose along her jaw and throat.

"If we're still together a year from now," she murmured, "I'm going to buy you a puppy."

"A black Lab?"

"Naturally."

He kissed her chin. "No puppies. My dog growing up came from a pound. That's what I want. A pre-owned dog. To match your pre-owned boyfriend."

She laughed. "Whatever you want."

He sighed, blinking at the far wall. "Eight hundred dollars a month. That's going to make such a difference, you have no idea."

She stroked his hair. "Good."

They'd have to be careful… They'd have to make sure the pressure of helping him stay afloat didn't leave Steph feeling trapped, should her feelings wane down the road. All the more reason to keep hustling, keep doing whatever it took.

"I won't let you down. I'm going to be that guy you've been wanting," he said, praying it was a promise he could keep. "It might take a couple years, but I can do that. Get to a point where I can support us both."

"I don't need to be *supported*. Not that way. I just want to feel like when things get too heavy for one person, the other's prepared to carry them, 'til they're back on their feet."

Patrick felt a funny pressure behind his eyes, and blinked it away.

"I just want a teammate, I guess," she added quietly. "Someone to grab the baton right before I collapse."

"I just hope I won't disappoint you." Or if he did, that it wouldn't come as a surprise, the next time.

"I don't know how you could."

"I don't have much to offer right now, aside from a financial burden."

She pushed up on her elbow and met his eyes. "You have tons to offer. You're kind, and talented, and hardworking. And handsome. And you have a beautiful home. And did I mention you're amazing at sex?"

He laughed, still feeling all vulnerable and dopey.

"And you cook really good macaroni and cheese," she added. "And you'd probably drive a hundred miles to help out a friend in the dead of night…and you'd drop everything you'd rather be doing on the off-chance there was work to be had."

"Yeah, I would."

"And any woman who doesn't think those things are enough…well, she's an idiot."

He thought she must mean his ex, until she averted her eyes, seeming to speak to his chest.

"I should have let you in right away."

"You were scared."

She nodded. "Yeah. I was."

"I bet you're not used to letting people see that."

"Not usually."

He pressed his lips to her forehead, again, again, again. For a long time they held each other, speaking only in soft, slowing breaths and idle caresses. Though it had been Steph's concern all along, Patrick suddenly registered how essential this feeling was—security. Support. He'd lost so much, so suddenly in his divorce. The uncertainty of being on his own with the mortgage had just blended into the whole. But now, with the prospect of help, of some kind of partnership and solidarity...

There was no telling how things would go, but just to know he could feel this again, with another person...

He squeezed her tight, amazed she cared for him this much. Enough to set aside her deepest fear to *partner* with him. To want to fall in love with him, in spite of those challenges. It made him feel stronger than he had in months. Wanted. Worthy.

"I won't let you down," he whispered again, believing it this time. Owning it in every cell in his body.

She smiled at him, and kissed his chin. "You couldn't if you tried."

* * * * *

COMING NEXT MONTH FROM

 HARLEQUIN®

 *Blaze*®

Available November 19, 2013

#775 COWBOYS & ANGELS
Sons of Chance
by Vicki Lewis Thompson

The last person ranch hand Trey Wheeler expects to meet at a ski lodge is the woman who saved him from a car crash. Elle Masterson is way more tempting than your average guardian angel—and Trey wants to be tempted....

#776 A SOLDIER'S CHRISTMAS
Uniformly Hot!
by Leslie Kelly, Joanne Rock and Karen Foley

When they come home for Christmas, three military heroes have visions in their heads of things far sexier than sugarplums. But the women they love want more than just one very good night....

#777 THE MIGHTY QUINNS: DEX
The Mighty Quinns
by Kate Hoffmann

When Irish news cameraman Dex Kennedy takes on a documentary project, he doesn't realize that the job will uncover some startling family secrets—and put him in the path of a sexy American producer who is all business. Except in the bedroom!

#778 NAUGHTY CHRISTMAS NIGHTS
by Tawny Weber

Romance vs sex? Designer Hailey North is determined her lacy lingerie will be the new holiday line at Rudolph's Department Stores. Gage Milano is providing competition with his hot leather look. But in the nights leading up to Christmas, things are heating up—between Hailey and Gage!

YOU CAN FIND MORE INFORMATION ON UPCOMING HARLEQUIN® TITLES, FREE EXCERPTS AND MORE AT WWW.HARLEQUIN.COM.

HBCNM1113

REQUEST YOUR FREE BOOKS!
2 FREE NOVELS PLUS 2 FREE GIFTS!

♥ HARLEQUIN®
Blaze®
red-hot reads!

YES! Please send me 2 FREE Harlequin® Blaze™ novels and my 2 FREE gifts (gifts are worth about $10). After receiving them, if I don't wish to receive any more books, I can return the shipping statement marked "cancel." If I don't cancel, I will receive 4 brand-new novels every month and be billed just $4.74 per book in the U.S. or $4.96 per book in Canada. That's a savings of at least 14% off the cover price. It's quite a bargain. Shipping and handling is just 50¢ per book in the U.S. and 75¢ per book in Canada.* I understand that accepting the 2 free books and gifts places me under no obligation to buy anything. I can always return a shipment and cancel at any time. Even if I never buy another book, the two free books and gifts are mine to keep forever.

150/350 HDN F4WC

Name _____ (PLEASE PRINT) _____

Address _____ Apt. # _____

City _____ State/Prov. _____ Zip/Postal Code _____

Signature (if under 18, a parent or guardian must sign) _____

Mail to the **Harlequin® Reader Service:**
IN U.S.A.: P.O. Box 1867, Buffalo, NY 14240-1867
IN CANADA: P.O. Box 609, Fort Erie, Ontario L2A 5X3

Want to try two free books from another line?
Call 1-800-873-8635 or visit www.ReaderService.com.

* Terms and prices subject to change without notice. Prices do not include applicable taxes. Sales tax applicable in N.Y. Canadian residents will be charged applicable taxes. Offer not valid in Quebec. This offer is limited to one order per household. Not valid for current subscribers to Harlequin Blaze books. All orders subject to credit approval. Credit or debit balances in a customer's account(s) may be offset by any other outstanding balance owed by or to the customer. Please allow 4 to 6 weeks for delivery. Offer available while quantities last.

Your Privacy—The Harlequin® Reader Service is committed to protecting your privacy. Our Privacy Policy is available online at www.ReaderService.com or upon request from the Harlequin Reader Service.

We make a portion of our mailing list available to reputable third parties that offer products we believe may interest you. If you prefer that we not exchange your name with third parties, or if you wish to clarify or modify your communication preferences, please visit us at www.ReaderService.com/consumerschoice or write to us at Harlequin Reader Service Preference Service, P.O. Box 9062, Buffalo, NY 14269. Include your complete name and address.

HB13R2

SPECIAL EXCERPT FROM

Enjoy this sneak peek of

The Mighty Quinns: Dex

by Kate Hoffmann, part of
The Mighty Quinns series in Harlequin Blaze!

Available November 19,
wherever Harlequin books are sold.

"We can't kiss again. We have to keep things strictly professional from here on out."

"Of course," Dex said. "I completely agree. And I can do that." He grabbed Marlie's hand and pulled her back down next to him.

They stared at each other for a long moment. "You're thinking about kissing me again, aren't you?" She sighed softly. "Maybe we just ought to do it again so we can move on."

Dex nodded. "You're right, it probably would help."

She drew a deep breath and forced a smile. "So, I guess you should just do it and get it over with."

"Right," Dex murmured.

Hell, he knew if he kissed her again, the attraction would never go away. It would just get worse. And then having to pretend that it didn't exist while they worked together would

HBEXP79781R

be pure torture. But he wasn't about to refuse her invitation. He wasn't a bloody eedjit.

Dex slipped his hand around her nape, his fingers tangling in her hair. He gently drew her close and touched his lips to hers. But the moment they made contact, he knew he was lost. A need so fierce, so overwhelming, surged up inside of him. He wanted to touch her, to kiss her, to tear her clothes off and make love to her until his body was exhausted and his mind was quiet.

Dex took a chance and pulled her even closer, his tongue teasing at her lips, searching for the warmth of her mouth and her unspoken surrender. When she opened beneath the assault, he groaned softly and drew her body on top of his, lying back on the sofa.

He needed this, a chance to clear his head of all the dark memories, all the twisted guilt that plagued his every waking minute. If he could just find some peace, if only for one night, maybe he could put his life back on track.

As their kiss grew more intense, Dex pulled her beneath him, desperate to feel her body against his. He stared down at her, his fingers brushing strands of hair from her face. Her lashes fluttered and the color was high in her cheeks. God, she was so beautiful, so perfect. The prospect of losing himself in her warmth was too tempting to deny.

She opened her eyes, their gazes meeting, and for a moment, he thought she was going to speak.

"What?" he murmured.

"I—I think that's enough," Marlie murmured.

"No," he whispered. "It's not nearly enough."

Pick up THE MIGHTY QUINNS: DEX by Kate Hoffmann, available November 19, wherever you buy Harlequin® Blaze® books.

Copyright © 2013 by Peggy A. Hoffmann

HBEXP79781R